Goooonnnnggggg!

Ivy plugged her fingers into her ears as the metallic vibrations echoed through the castle. She had thought she was having a nightmare. She pinched herself, but the resounding noise still rang out. *It's . . . it's. . .* She suddenly recognised the sound. *The gong!* That could mean only one thing in Transylvania. *A duel!*

Sink your fangs into these:

MY SISTER THE VAMPIRE

Switched

Fangtastic!

Revamped!

Vampalicious

Take Two

Love Bites

Lucky Break

Star Style

Twin Spins!

Date with Destiny

Flying Solo

Stake Out!

Double Disaster!

Flipping Out

Secrets and Spies

Fashion Frightmare

MY BROTHER THE WEREWOLF

Cry Wolf!

Puppy Love!

Howl-oween!

Tail Spin

EGMONT

With special thanks to Chandler Craig

For Emily and Kelley, for listening

EGMONT

We bring stories to life

My Sister the Vampire: Date with Destiny first published
in Great Britain 2012
by Egmont UK Limited
The Yellow Building, 1 Nicholas Road, London W11 4AN

Created by Working Partners Limited, London WC1X 9HH

ISBN 978 1 4052 5985 9

5 7 9 10 8 6 4

www.egmont.co.uk

A CIP catalogue record for this title is available from the British Library

Typeset by Avon DataSet Ltd, Bidford on Avon, Warwickshire
Printed and bound in Great Britain by the CPI Group

49532/5

Chapter One

The horror . . . the horror!

Olivia stood in the doorway of her vampire twin's bedroom staring at one of the scariest sights she'd ever seen. Black v-necks, skinny jeans and trendy boots were strewn over the plush red carpeting of Ivy's room. None of them was even remotely close to a suitcase.

'Ivy Vega!' Olivia exclaimed, smacking her forehead. 'We leave for Transylvania *tomorrow*! As in twenty-four hours from now.'

Ivy was sitting cross-legged on the floor. She glanced up from her laptop where she was busy browsing the Vorld Vide Veb, the vampire version of the internet. 'Oops.' She shrugged. 'I got a little distracted.' She held her finger and thumb a couple of centimetres apart.

'Oops' is right, thought Olivia. *How is Ivy possibly going to be ready in time? She hasn't even begun packing!* The two of them had received personal invitations to Tessa and Prince Alex's royal wedding. There were outfit choices to be made and shoe decisions and . . . Olivia shook herself. This wasn't the time to panic; this was the time for *action*.

She scooped up two limp T-shirts. 'In case you've forgotten, you have a very important interview coming up at a certain fancy finishing school for vampires.' Olivia frowned down at her twin, mock stern. As part of the vampire elite, Ivy's vampire powers were getting stronger by the day now that she was getting older. Their grandparents, the Count and Countess, had come over to Franklin Grove especially to persuade

Ivy that she should learn to control her powers at Wallachia Academy – Transylvania's most exclusive vampire school.

'Chill, my ultra-organised twin.' Ivy rolled her heavily kohled eyes. 'I've started packing.'

'Taking your clothes out of your closet and dropping them on the floor does *not* equal packing.' Olivia held up Ivy's rumpled T-shirts as evidence. 'It equals a mess.' She started folding the T-shirts into neat squares. She couldn't help herself; the chaos was beginning to stress her out. 'Right,' she said. 'I'm going to have to take over this whole operation. Suitcase?' she asked, as if she were a surgeon requesting her scalpel.

Ivy pointed at a turned-over suitcase jutting halfway out of the closet. 'See? At least I got it half-out.'

Olivia picked her way through her sister's scattered belongings, trying not to step on the clothes – she certainly didn't want to have to iron too! In moments, she was creating a neat stack of jeans and tops inside Ivy's bag just as she had done with her own not so darkly coloured clothes yesterday. She looked over her shoulder at Ivy, who had returned to her computer. On-screen, Olivia spotted the Wallachia Academy crest with its two bats on either side of a blood-red shield. Very vampire-esque.

Olivia was half aware that she was folding clothes increasingly slowly – she just couldn't help staring at the screen, even though she knew it was rude to watch over someone's shoulder. The pictures of Wallachia Academy showed happy-looking teenagers tossing Frisbees on perfectly manicured lawns. Girls sat beneath trees to read in the shade. And the boys, Olivia had to admit, looked completely drop dead. Wallachia Academy seemed more like a teenage resort than the stuffy private school that her twin sister was dreading so much.

Ivy must have sensed her looking because she glanced up from the screen.

'Socks!' Olivia blurted to cover up her snooping. 'You can't go to Wallachia Academy without socks!' She frowned. 'In fact, I'm not sure many of these clothes are suitable. You're going to be mixing with Transylvanian high society.' Olivia held up a black T-shirt with the words 'Silent Night, Scary Night' printed in a spooky white font. 'I mean, *seriously*?'

Ivy snatched the T-shirt from Olivia's grasp. 'I sleep in that!'

Olivia crinkled her nose. 'Even so.' She flung wide the doors to Ivy's closet. 'You need to wear your best stuff if you're going to impress at your interview.' She started flipping through the hangers. 'A nice dress – black, obviously – will do the trick.' Olivia pulled out a simple shift and another long-sleeved wrap dress. Ivy's fashion sense leaned a bit darker than Olivia's preferred parade of pink, but her sister still always managed to look completely vampire-vogue. *So what's she doing packing a bunch of uncoordinated outfits?*

'These are old, though,' Olivia continued. 'What we need is an emergency shopping trip. I know! I'll call Sophia. She can meet us at the mall. And –'

'*Olivia!*'

Olivia slumped on to the bed, scattered with goth band T-shirts. 'I'm overdoing it, aren't I?'

Ivy nodded, a sympathetic smile on her face.

'I just want you to make the most of this awesome opportunity and I don't want you to think I'm going to be upset at the thought of not having you around for a while.' Olivia stretched the corners of her mouth into the widest grin possible. 'See? I'm totally OK with it all.'

Ivy giggled. 'OK? You're zipping around like a bumble bee who's had too much sugar. Plus,' Ivy went on, leaning forwards, 'I haven't decided

I'm going. I'm checking it out. That's all.'

Olivia lifted an eyebrow. 'Now don't make me go super-bossy for real. This is the kind of thing other vamp kids would eat a vegetarian sandwich for. If you really do want to go to Wallachia, then nothing in Franklin Grove should stop you.'

'But –'

'Brendan and I will still be here when you get back. He adores you; he'd wait a lifetime.' Olivia picked up a framed picture of Ivy, Olivia and Brendan making goofy faces in the movie-theatre photo booth and tossed it in her twin's bag. *Just in case.*

Ivy nodded, twisting her mouth as if she was trying to think up another objection. 'I still don't like the thought of you being left on your own. Especially after . . .'

Olivia's muscles went rigid and Ivy froze mid sentence. It was clear she'd been about to say the J-word, which had been officially erased from their vocabulary. Although Olivia and her Hollywood boyfriend, Jackson, had shared a swoon-worthy slow dance at the recent school prom, it had been really hard to say goodbye afterwards, when he'd had to return to filming. *Like, really hard.* The two of them had tried to Skype and phone as often as they could, but with his long hours on set and Olivia's social life, they'd kept missing each other. The writers' strike was still on in Hollywood, but Jackson had agreed to join some filming in Europe for a small, independent set of film-makers – to give his career more credibility, he'd told Olivia – and now he was even busier.

'We need to make this easier on ourselves,' Jackson had said, during their last conversation. 'Let's agree not to be in touch until we can meet face-to-face. Deal?'

'Deal,' Olivia had agreed, even though it had made her heart twist. Anything had to be better than the torture of missed phone calls and terse conversations. Since that last discussion, they hadn't spoken, and Olivia had banned everyone from talking to her about Jackson or even saying his name. It seemed harsh, she knew, but it was the only way to save herself from going half crazy pining for him.

Hollywood plus Franklin Grove did not equal an easy relationship, it turned out.

Olivia chewed her lip, shifting on the bed. She could feel tears starting to pool in the corners of her eyes. *Great*, she thought. Just as she was trying to convince Ivy that she was super-OK with her leaving, here she was turning into a blubbering mess.

'You know what?' Ivy jumped up, clapping her hands. 'We *should* pack!'

Olivia laughed at her sister's attempt to act like her personal cheerleader. She still felt as if she had a boulder in her stomach, but at least the awkward silence was broken. Her tears spilled over on to her cheeks. *At least Ivy's pretending not to notice*, she thought. Ivy always knew just the best way to behave around Olivia, especially when it came to affairs of the heart.

The two of them threw themselves down by the suitcase and got to work. Olivia was a machine, grabbing, folding and packing. She was so consumed with her task, she could almost forget that she no longer actually spoke to her handsome celebrity boyfriend.

Olivia reached for a jumper and felt a sharp tug on the fabric from the other end. She let go, scared it would rip.

'*Waaaah!*' Ivy toppled backwards, hitting the ground with a thump. Olivia hadn't even noticed Ivy was holding it too!

'Are you OK?' Olivia asked, through sniggers that snuck past her lips. After a moment, she gave up trying to hide her laughter – at least the gloomy mood had been zapped. Olivia pulled her sister back upright, still giggling.

'What's so funny?' asked a voice from behind them.

Ivy and Olivia span round. On the screen of Ivy's computer, the Wallachia web site had been replaced by a real-time image of Georgia Huntingdon. Georgia's thin face peered out at them through artsy reading glasses. 'Well?' asked Georgia.

Olivia's eyes were wide. She'd never seen a vamp use the Lonely Echo online phone programme, but that had to be what Georgia was using to contact them! The question was, why was *VAMP* magazine's best journalist getting in touch in the first place? Ivy and Olivia crowded in front of the screen.

'Um, hi there,' said Ivy, adjusting her video cam so that they were both in the frame. 'We were just laughing because . . . Well, it seemed funny at the time.'

'Never mind.' Georgia's ringlet curls swished across her shoulders. 'I'm glad I caught you. Listen, I'm in the hospital.'

Ivy gasped. 'What happened?'

Georgia lifted her arm and a thick, black cast appeared on the screen. 'I broke my wrist on a skiing vacation in Aspen.' She shook her head. 'Now I get to walk around for ten weeks with this as my accessory.'

Olivia groaned. She could just imagine how much it would pain the magazine editor to be stuck with an ungainly cast. *I bet she's not even allowed to accessorise it with diamanté.*

Ivy shuddered. 'Sounds painful. You can count me out of the whole skiing thing. I'm never going – too dangerous.'

'Yes, it can be . . . quite treacherous,' Georgia said. She suddenly started busying herself with stirring sugar into a cup of coffee on a side table beside her chair.

'Was it a black slope?' Olivia asked, shuddering. 'I've heard that they're terrifying.'

'Like sheets of glass,' Ivy agreed.

'Um . . .' Olivia noticed that Georgia now had two pink spots on her cheeks. 'The ice was very bad, I hear.' Her voice had gone almost as soft as a whisper.

The twins shared a glance. Even Olivia had to admit, she felt the prickle of something not being quite right.

'You hear?' Ivy repeated. 'You mean you don't know? How did you break your wrist exactly?'

Georgia slammed her coffee cup down so that black liquid spilt over her cashmere skirt.

'Now, really, girls! Who is the journalist here? You or me? These probing questions really aren't necessary.' She called to someone off-screen whom the twins couldn't see. 'David! Bring me a napkin!' She was busy wiping down her skirt.

Olivia felt laughter bubbling up inside of her.

'Georgia? Did you even make it out on to the slopes?'

Their friend gave a deep sigh and gazed up at them. 'All right, all right, I'll admit it. I slipped while I was putting my ski boots on in the hotel room. Can you believe that?' Georgia smacked herself on the forehead, knocking her head with the giant plaster cast. She rolled her eyes. 'Wrong hand.'

Ivy scooted out of view of the computer webcam, squeezing her hand over her mouth. She tried to cover up her snort of laughter with a fake sneeze.

Olivia's shoulders shook too but she managed not to laugh. 'Excuse my sister.' She shot Ivy a meaningful look. 'She's recovering from a very *sudden* cold.'

'Sorry, Georgia,' said Ivy, composing herself as she stepped in front of the screen again. 'You were saying?'

Georgia rolled her eyes. 'Yes, very funny, I'm sure. But with my injury, I can't cover the Vampire Royal Wedding in Transylvania.'

Olivia furrowed her eyebrows.

Georgia must have noticed her confused look. 'A journalist can't write with a hairline fracture in her arm.' That did sound unpleasant, but Olivia still didn't understand what it had to do with them. 'But it's OK,' continued Georgia. 'I have the best back-up plan. Why don't *you two* cover the wedding on my behalf?'

'Cover the wedding?' Olivia and Ivy asked in unison.

'You would be roving reporters for *VAMP* magazine. I know you already have invitations, so it's perfect. A young, fresh perspective.' She paused. 'So – how does that sound?'

Ivy wasn't laughing any more. A chance at being a real journalist! Olivia knew how much that would mean to her sister. And *VAMP* magazine was sold in practically every BloodMart in the country. It was a huge opportunity. 'Are you serious?'

'Dead,' replied Georgia. Olivia could see her personal assistant, David, in the background, smoothing cushions on a chaise longue. Clearly, it was nearly time for the star journalist's afternoon nap.

'Will you do it, darlings?' she asked, as she climbed on to the chaise longue and David arranged an eye mask over her face.

'We'd love to!' the girls said together. Georgia gave a smile of acknowledgement and the window vanished from the screen.

'I feel like bats are fluttering inside my tummy,' Ivy murmured. Olivia knew this might be her sister's big break into the journalism world. '*Ivy Vega reporting from Transylvania* . . .' Ivy turned to stare at Olivia, her eyes wide. 'I like the sound of that!'

* * *

'It gets even better,' said Ivy. 'Olivia and I actually get to work together. Olivia's going to take the photos and advise me on all the names of the dresses and things.' She had her elbows propped on a table at the Meat and Greet diner, leaning in as she relayed every detail of her conversation with Georgia to Sophia and Brendan. 'Isn't that the most A-positive thing to happen?'

Brendan smiled, though Ivy noticed that it didn't quite reach his eyes. He glanced away and Ivy paused while Sophia slipped out of the booth for some fresh napkins.

'Everything's OK, isn't it?' she asked him, once Sophia was out of earshot. 'You're sure you're OK with me going?'

Brendan brushed a lock of hair from her eyes. 'Of course I'm sure. I encouraged you, didn't I? It's just . . . I'd hoped *this* would be the most A-positive thing to happen to you.'

He drew a small velvet box from the back pocket of his jeans and put it down on the table between Ivy and himself. 'It's a little going-away gift.'

'Oh, Brendan, you shouldn't have . . .' Ivy said.

'Well, in that case!' Brendan started to take the box back, but Ivy snatched it up before he had the chance. They both laughed.

'Open it,' Brendan said softly.

The hinges creaked as Ivy prised back the satin-lined lid. Inside was a small jewelled brooch in the shape of the letter 'I' in swirly lettering.

'It's perfect,' Ivy breathed. She wasn't obsessed with jewellery in the way Olivia was, but this was understated and personal. She couldn't have asked for anything more.

'I'd tell you you're the perfect boyfriend, but I don't want your head to get too big,' Ivy said, as she pinned the brooch to her top. Sophia arrived back at their table, her eyes wide.

'Brendan – did you buy Ivy the perfect gift?' Ivy grinned as Sophia sat back down.

'You sure you want to go?' she asked Ivy, nodding at Brendan. 'You're really going to leave this guy behind?'

Brendan placed a hand over Ivy's. 'I wouldn't have it any other way. Me and royal weddings . . . I can take them or leave them. Ivy and Olivia will have a riot without me.'

And afterwards? Ivy thought. What if she didn't come back? She shook herself. Some things weren't worth thinking about on days as happy as this.

The Meat and Greet was busy. Near the counter Olivia was standing with her best friend, Camilla Edmunson, who was adjusting her purple beret and yelling 'Cut!' Camilla was in the middle of making a short film that had become a full-on summer project. Olivia and Ivy had been offered acting roles, but the Transylvania trip had interfered. Not that Ivy minded; Olivia was more the thespian of the family. Much more! Ivy was not exactly natural on stage or in front of the camera. She remembered Camilla using the words 'wooden' and 'painful' when she'd given her feedback after her last acting experience.

Ivy watched the scene, which seemed to involve a brightly costumed alien girl and a robo-boy on a date. Ivy hoped it wouldn't remind Olivia of her performance opposite Jackson in Romezog and Julietron – also a Camilla Edmunson production.

'Oh, X3219,' said the alien girl in a strange, high-pitched voice. 'I'm going to miss you!'

Robo-boy attempted to wrap alien girl in a stiff-armed hug, but couldn't seem to figure out how to embrace her while keeping his elbows bent at right angles.

'Cut! Cut!' Camilla yelled, before putting the

actors back into their original places. 'Try that part again.'

Back at the table, Brendan was busy building a fort out of French fries and Ivy couldn't help but wonder: *Is Brendan really not bothered that I'm so excited to go to Transylvania? Even a little bit?* Surely he knew how much she'd miss him. If only Ivy could promise that she'd be back soon. But the truth was, she had no idea if she'd be returning to Franklin Grove. *Maybe it would be best if I don't talk about it quite so much, just in case.*

Then, she did something very un-Ivy. Reaching for Brendan's hand under the table, she wove her fingers through his and gave his hand a squeeze. Fortunately, he'd already wiped his hands on a napkin so that his fingers weren't covered in salt and grease from the fries.

'I'm going to miss you,' she murmured, forcing herself not to blush.

'I'm so jealous!' A voice from across the table

made the couple jump apart, before Brendan had a chance to answer. Sophia had caught the Transylvania bug and madly wanted to be catching a plane there herself. *There goes not talking about it*, Ivy thought. 'I would love the chance to go to your home country. All the history, the great shopping, plus vamp boys everywhere!'

That is so not helping! Ivy kicked Sophia's shins under the table. 'Ouch!' she yelped, reaching down to rub her leg. But at least she had the sense to change topic.

'You know where else I want to go? Paris! I'd love to go to Paris!'

'*Oui, oui*! Me too! Hey, nice brooch!' said a familiar voice. Looking round, Ivy saw Olivia approaching the table.

Sophia started ticking places off on her fingers. 'And Rome and London and . . .' She threw up her hands. 'It's not fair! You get to go to Transylvania for the second time. *And* I can't so much as go on Twitter without seeing another update from some fabulous film set in Europe that Jackson has posted.'

Ivy sucked in her breath, not daring to look at the expression on her sister's face. Even though it was jam-packed, the Meat and Greet suddenly felt still and silent as the grave.

Sophia obviously hasn't received the memo about the J-word, Ivy thought. *Doesn't she know Olivia can't even talk* to *her boyfriend, never mind* about *him!*

Chapter Two

She said the J-word!

Olivia took a long gulp of lemonade, trying desperately to keep her face neutral. She stared out of the window so Sophia wouldn't see her eyes becoming glassy. Wrong move. The first thing she spotted was a boy and girl about her age. They were walking down the street, holding hands and gazing at each other as if the rest of the world didn't exist. *Just like Jackson and I used to*, she thought, a pain starting in her chest. *When we were together. When we actually talked. Look away, look away!* No problem, she would just keep her eyes in the Meat and Greet. That should be simple enough. After all, there were plenty of people to distract her.

She turned her face back towards the people inside, trying to focus on the restaurant and its familiar red and black decor. Another bad move. Behind Brendan, Olivia saw an older couple sharing a milkshake out of two straws. She inched to the left, so that Brendan's head would block her view, but now Camilla's alien-robot couple was in full sight and the two actors were in the middle of an awkward, but sweet, alien-robot kiss.

'What is this, Couples Day?' Olivia muttered under her breath. It seemed that everyone in the world was happy except for her. Not that she would deny anyone else their romantic moment, but why did she have to be so obviously *alone*?

'Um, Olivia?' she heard Sophia saying. Olivia's head jerked up as she realised that the other three people at the table had stopped talking and were staring at her.

'Er . . .' They'd obviously picked up on her unhappiness. *Oh no! I didn't mean to invite everyone to my pity party!* She forced herself to grin and smoothed her hair. 'What?' she asked, sitting up straight. 'I'm fine!' Ivy eyed her from across the table. 'I *am*.' Olivia nodded vigorously. 'Jackson's busy working and I'm totally happy for him. He made the right choice. He has to look after his career. I'm fine. One-hundred-and-ten per cent fine.' She wanted to crawl under the table. *Note to self: People who are fine don't say they're fine three times!*

'Brendan, are there any souvenirs you want from Transylvania?' asked Ivy, switching topics. Olivia really did have the best twin on the planet.

Brendan rumpled his dark hair. 'I don't know,' he mumbled. 'Whatever you think I'll like. Surprise me!' Olivia noticed that he seemed distracted.

'I know!' Olivia bounced up from the booth. 'How about I buy a round of ice cream for everyone? It'll be a parting gift. My treat!

Brendan, can you help me carry them back?' She gestured for him to follow her up to the counter.

Brendan loped alongside her, taking a spot in line behind the boy playing the blue robot. Nearby, Camilla knelt with her bulky camera on one shoulder, shooting the lens up towards the actor-robot. 'Just act naturally,' she directed. 'You're a robot in need of some oil. *Feel* the creakiness in your joints. *Need* the oilcan. Action!'

The robot stepped up to the cashier, his words coming out short and choppy. 'Ex-cuse me,' said robo-boy, trying to sound electronic. 'But may I have some oil to mend my wound-ed heart valve?' Robo-boy pressed a rigid hand to his chest.

The cashier looked around the robot to Brendan and Olivia. She screwed up her face and twirled one finger at the side of her head. 'Loopy!'

Olivia pretended she hadn't heard, and instead eyed the menu above the cashier's head and the vamp-tastic names of the ice creams: *Count Cherry*

Chocula; Batty Blackberry; Crypt's Coconut. She elbowed Brendan as they waited for their turn to be served. 'Are you OK with Ivy going away?' she asked. 'You can be honest with me, you know.'

Brendan rubbed his ribs. 'Ouch! Sure, I'm OK. Whatever's good for Ivy is good for me.'

Olivia rolled her eyes. Brendan was a vampire. He probably hadn't even felt her jab. 'If you're trying to make a big show of being "cool" with this trip, you don't have to, you know. It's OK to be a bit sad!'

Brendan stared at his black shoelaces. 'Let's just take it one step at a time.'

'Brendan Daniels, don't give me the brave face.'

Brendan dug the toe of one trainer into the ground. 'I'm just trying to do what's best.'

Olivia stepped in front of Brendan, turning her back to the ice-cream counter and facing towards robo-boy, who was still busy fumbling with his lines. 'Give it more *passion*!' she heard

Camilla tell him. 'Really commit to the part.'

'Brendan, I may be small – and a bunny – but if this ever gets too much for you, I want you to know you can confide in me. You can confide in Ivy! She cares a lot for you and would only want you to be honest about how you're feeling.'

Brendan took a step back. 'Thanks, Olivia.' He swept his hand through his hair, suddenly looking a little worried. 'But please don't say anything to Ivy, OK?'

Olivia's eyes flitted quickly in her sister's direction. Ivy was staring at the pair of them with her head cocked. She was clearly getting the sense that something was up.

Olivia smiled sweetly, as if to say, *Everything's fine.* Then she turned back to Brendan. 'I promise. We'll look out for each other whilst she's away.' She held out her pinky.

Brendan stared. 'I'm not pinky swearing, Olivia. I'm a dude!'

Olivia lifted her eyebrows and jutted her chin, waiting.

'Fine,' said Brendan, letting his head hang in defeat. He locked pinkies with her and shook. 'I promise too. Happy?'

'Very.' Olivia stepped up to the front of the line and rested her hand on the cool metal of the Meat and Greet counter, where a pale goth girl with a black apron was waiting with a pen and pad. 'Two Dark Chocolate Delights and two Scrumptious Strawberry ice-cream cones, please.'

The girl smiled through dark-red lips and Olivia could just make out where the cashier's dazzling white fangs had been filed. 'Four cones, coming right up!'

While they waited, Olivia waved to Camilla, who was letting her actors 'take five'. 'It looks like the shoot's going well,' Olivia said, as her friend approached.

Camilla tucked a clipboard under her arm.

'It is.' She lowered her voice. 'But it would be so much better with you and . . .' Olivia felt her heart do a back-flip – and not a happy one. *Not the J-word, not the J-word.* Camilla opened her mouth and then closed it. 'Um, yeah . . .' Camilla cleared her throat, 'with *you* in it.'

Olivia quickly fixed a big smile on her face. As if on cue, the cashier handed over four cones. Brendan took two, Olivia the other two. As she reached for them, she smiled at Camilla. 'I hope the rest of the filming goes well,' said Olivia, refusing to let her smile slip. 'Sorry I can't be here for it.' *I'm fine*, she repeated. *Totally fine.*

If I keep telling myself that, perhaps one day I'll believe it.

Ivy just did not get Chinese orchestral music. The low-pitched strings and relentless drums were anything but relaxing. Unfortunately that was what Olivia's adoptive dad, Mr Abbott, insisted on listening to as he drove Olivia and Ivy to the airport before their long flight to Transylvania.

Mr Abbott hummed along with the CD. 'It's very Zen, don't you think?'

More like very annoying, thought Ivy.

Horatio, her grandparents' hulking butler, was squished between the girls in the back seat, his knees pulled up to his chest. His sleek black tuxedo jacket was stretched tight across his back and his suit trousers were hiked high above his ankles, revealing bright-red socks. Ivy's grandparents had been summoned back to Transylvania to help prepare for the wedding, but they'd left Horatio behind to help the girls pack. 'You really ought to have let one of us sit in the middle,' said Olivia, her knees squashed against the door.

Horatio peered down his nose. 'I would not hear of it, Miss Olivia. I am here, as always, to serve.' Ivy snorted. Right now, Horatio was only serving to block the air conditioning!

Charles Vega, the twins' bio-dad, was sitting up front next to Mr Abbott. 'It's very kind of you to drive us to the airport,' he said. 'We won't forget this.'

Horatio shifted his weight in the back seat, hands fidgeting. He had repeatedly asked Olivia's dad if he could drive, but Mr Abbott wouldn't hear a word of it. Horatio hated anyone else being the chauffeur.

He hated anyone else doing *any* work.

'Don't be silly,' said Mr Abbott, tapping the wheel in time to the drumbeats. 'You all are extended family. And you know what they say: *the strength of a nation derives from the integrity of the home.*' In the reflection of the rear-view mirror Ivy saw Mr Abbott's eyebrows lift. 'Can anyone name that quote?'

The twins looked at each other blankly.

'Confucius,' said Charles and Horatio in unison.

Mr Abbott nodded. 'Impressive.'

Great. The next thing Ivy knew, her dad would be practising yoga on the front lawn too. She leaned forwards, trying to get Olivia's attention – someone who could share her pain – but Olivia's chin rested on her fist as she stared intently out of the window. Ivy chewed her lip. It wasn't like Olivia to bottle things up. *Dark and stormy is usually more* my *style.* The twins were becoming more and more like each other and Ivy wasn't sure that was entirely a good thing. Olivia was supposed to be the perky one – the Yin to Ivy's Yang.

Ivy's phone pinged from inside her black studded bag – a text! She plunged her hands inside, digging through the mess of lipstick, movie stubs, and spare tubes of Pale Beauty, hoping it was a message from Brendan. She pulled the phone out and thumbed the touch screen.

Hope you have a safe flight! V-Love, Sophia.

Ivy's heart sank. Not that it wasn't a nice text;

it just wasn't the one she wanted. She clicked out of the message without responding and looked at her phone's wallpaper screen – a picture of her and Brendan making silly faces. Brendan had his cheeks puffed out and he was scratching his head like a chimpanzee, and she had sucked her cheeks into a ridiculous fish-face. *We look so happy.* She stroked the brooch that she was wearing on her top. *I hope we're still that happy when I get back.*

Ivy shoved the phone back into her bag, trying not to think about how *fine* he had seemed at the Meat and Greet. How unconcerned about the time they would be spending apart. Ivy knew Brendan well enough to understand that it was probably just his way of coping, but she couldn't help feeling a little hurt. Of course, she had wanted him to be OK with her trip to Transylvania – but there was such a thing as being *too* OK with being separated from your girlfriend for a week or two. Maybe longer.

As the wheels of the car edged up to the kerb at the airport, Ivy frowned to herself. Brendan Daniels was not supposed to behave like a dumb guy from a stupid teen bunny show.

Ivy's boyfriend was supposed to be different.

Charles shut the boot of Mr Abbott's car. He surveyed the luggage piled on the pavement as a plane roared overhead. 'I think that's everything.'

'Literally,' Ivy muttered, her eyebrows raised. *Leave it to Olivia to pack our entire wardrobes!*

Olivia smiled sheepishly. 'Hey, a girl's got to have options.'

Police officers were directing traffic and luggage wheels slid across the pavement with regular thuds. The terminal was a hub of activity.

Mr Abbott extended his hand to Horatio, who looked at it, blinking. Ivy stifled a giggle. Horatio's giant hand daintily gripped Mr Abbott's fingers and he gave them a gentle shake. Poor Horatio really did not know how to handle being treated like an equal.

'Well then,' Mr Abbott said. 'I wouldn't want you all to miss your flight.'

Olivia reached up to give her adoptive dad a long hug. 'I'll miss you. Take care of Mom, OK?'

Mr Abbott kissed her on top of the head. 'Would you like me to come in with you?' he asked.

Olivia shook her head. 'That's OK. Horatio can help us.' Ivy thought she saw Horatio perk up with that comment. The Lazar family butler took the phrase 'aim to please' to a whole new level!

'Right, well . . . In that case, I might just make my tai chi class.' He started to smile, then threw his arms wide. 'Oh, who am I kidding? Who cares about tai chi? Come here and give me a hug!' He swooped the twins up in his arms, crushing them tight to his chest. Eventually, he pulled away, his face red. 'I know I shouldn't get emotional. It's only for a week.'

'Not to worry.' Charles cleared his throat and shook Mr Abbott's hand. 'Horatio is anxious to lend a helping hand, I'm sure.' The already massive butler straightened up – so tall, Ivy feared a plane might fly into his head. Even by vamp standards, Horatio was pretty freaky.

Mr Abbott had recovered his composure. He put his palms together as if praying and bowed. 'In that case, I bid you, *yī lù shùn fēng*.'

'*Xiè xiè*,' replied Horatio, bowing in return.

'Bye, Dad!' Olivia turned to wave one last time to Mr Abbott and then the four of them trooped through the whooshing sliding glass doors and into the airport.

'Horatio, I didn't know you spoke Chinese,' Charles remarked.

He bowed slightly, with a faint smile. 'There is a lot you do not know about me, Master Karl. Now if you'll excuse me . . .' He took Ivy and Olivia's duffel bags. 'I want to make myself useful at last.'

All around them, passengers were bustling about, dragging suitcases and sprinting to gates. Ticket personnel were calling for the next person in line. Departure and arrival times scrolled down the monitors. Ivy's chest squeezed as she saw a young couple kissing goodbye at the entrance to the security line. She would have felt much better if Brendan had given her one last kiss before she'd left, but it was too late now. She would have to wait until she got back – whenever that was.

She trailed behind her father. 'The Lazar family, checking in,' Ivy heard him say at the ticket desk, but she was hardly paying attention. Olivia handed her a boarding pass with her name stamped on it. The check-in, the walk through the giant metal detectors at security, the approach to the terminal – they all passed in one muffled blur as if everything was happening at a distance.

'Ivy?' Lillian tapped her shoulder, her gold-

and-blue eyes searching Ivy's face. 'Are you looking forward to the trip?'

Whoa, where did Lillian come from? Ivy hadn't even noticed her joining up with them at the gate.

Ivy blinked and channelled her best Olivia impression. 'Absolutely!' she replied, a peppy smile plastered on her lips.

Actually, Ivy *was* pleased that Lillian was coming along as her father's date. She and Olivia agreed that the two vamps made a perfect pair. Plus, Lillian always let Ivy borrow her most on-trend vamp make-up. As a Hollywood insider, Lillian had Midnight Marauder eyeshadow *months* before it was out in the shops!

'Is everything OK?' Lillian leaned on the armrest of one of the grey plastic chairs in Departures. She wore a deep-plum tunic over black leggings. Her fashionable flats tapped the floor. Olivia was on the other side of her, flipping through a tabloid magazine. *Which is not that sensible if she's trying to avoid thinking about the J-word*, Ivy thought.

Ivy straightened up. 'Sure, yeah, I'm fine. Everything's totally fine.' She sounded like Olivia! The truth was that Ivy's head felt fuzzy and she couldn't seem to focus on what was going on in the airport. The only thing she *was* aware of was the object in the pocket of her jeans – her cell phone.

Her *very silent* cell phone.

Then, as if Ivy had psychic powers, she felt a tingle against her leg. *Please be Brendan, please be Brendan.* She wriggled her phone out from her pocket.

'Brendan?' she asked, breathless.

Her boyfriend's slow, warm voice came over the line. 'Hey! I was worried I'd miss you! I was in the mall and couldn't get phone reception. I've come outside to call.'

At last, a real smile stretched across Ivy's lips,

so wide it hurt her cheeks. 'Thank you,' she said, wishing she could wrap him in a hug. 'Save a spot at the Meat and Greet for me?'

'You bet. Have a safe flight. And, Ivy? I didn't get a chance to say it yesterday: *I'll miss you too.*'

Ivy hung up the phone and stashed it in her hand luggage. She really did have the perfect boyfriend.

Over the intercom a woman called, 'Boarding all rows for flight seven zero three to Transylvania. All rows, boarding now.'

'Eek!' Olivia squealed. 'That's us!' She looped her arm through Ivy's. 'You have your ticket?'

Ivy waved it in reply. The flight attendant scanned her ticket and before she knew it she was stepping on to the plush Transylvania Air jumbo jet, with its crimson aisles and red velour seats. Ivy made her way towards their seats in first class. *7B . . . 7B . . .* There it was. She tossed her bag on to her empty aisle seat. *B for Brendan.*

He'd done everything he could to make her feel good about this trip. One day there'd be a seat on a plane bringing her back to him. But for now . . . *Translyvania here I come!* she thought, clicking the seatbelt shut over her hips. *You'd better be ready for me!*

Chapter Three

First class or not, Olivia was thrilled to be off the flight. She was so jet-lagged her arms and legs felt as if they were encased in concrete. It seemed like every other in-flight film had starred the J-word. Olivia hadn't known he'd *made* that many movies. *The universe must be out to get me – or, at least, the airline is!*

And to make matters worse, she had ended up watching some horror flick called *Fangs At Dusk* just to avoid anything that would remind her of *him*, but that movie had been totally scary, and now she kept expecting blood-sucking vampires to jump out at her at any moment! *Don't be ridiculous*, Olivia told herself. None of the vamps she knew would ever do silly things like that. *Ivy would probably eat a whole loaf of garlic bread before wearing a cape!*

Olivia turned her attention back to Horatio. He was behind the wheel of the luxury Cadillac he'd left in long-term parking at the Transylvanian airport. His chauffeur's cap was back on his head and Olivia could see a big grin stretching across his face. She guessed Horatio was happy to be home in more ways than one. He was way more comfortable when he was taking care of people.

In fact, Olivia thought, maybe the butler was a little *too* much in his comfort zone, because they were going so fast on the windy country roads that it felt like they might fly off at any moment. It was worst for Olivia: she was sitting in the front passenger seat, while her bio-dad and Lillian were in the back with Ivy.

She watched as the needle on the speedometer

climbed. Were Lillian and Charles concerned? She glanced in the rear-view mirror, but the couple were sitting pressed close together as Charles murmured in Lillian's ear – small tidbits about the scenery that was whizzing by.

Olivia took a deep breath. She knew Horatio's vampire reflexes made him a safer driver than any non-vamp on the road, but she couldn't help clutching the door handle for dear life. She was only human, after all!

Thankfully, the view outside the Cadillac window served as the perfect distraction. The rolling hills were like green waves speckled with red-roofed houses, and the forest that lined the highway was a bright emerald. Olivia had never seen so much vibrant green. She bet her botany teacher, Mr Strain, would be very impressed with all the plant-life here. A cluster of stone towers peeked out from a forest of towering pines, and Olivia remembered their last visit, when her bio-dad had pointed it out as the castle where the real Dracula used to live. The Transylvanian countryside was among the most beautiful in the world. *Honestly, Ivy would be lucky to stay here!*

Minutes later, Horatio's Cadillac whooshed through the Lazars' gates and between the pillars topped with creepy stone gargoyles.

Somebody's been watching a few too many car chases, Olivia thought, rubbing her belly and concentrating on not getting car sick.

The Cadillac zipped up the long, winding driveway of the Gothic mansion where Ivy and Olivia's grandparents lived. It was still hard to believe that she, Olivia Abbott, was descended from vampire aristocracy. How posh! How chic! *How completely weird.*

'It's lovely,' said Lillian, peering out of the window at the ivy-covered walls and pointed turrets. 'Even better than I'd imagined!' Lillian looked down at her outfit, smoothing her tunic.

'Oh dear, I'm all wrinkled. Do you think Horatio has something to help?'

'Don't worry,' Olivia leaned in and whispered. 'You look great.'

Horatio honked the horn, which played a sombre bar of a song that sounded vaguely familiar to Olivia. She giggled. 'What kind of honk was *that*? It was Mozart, right?'

Charles swished his fingers through the air as if conducting an invisible orchestra. 'Excellent! That was a snippet from the "Lacrimosa" passage of Mozart's *Requiem*.'

Olivia shook her head. 'I can't believe I actually got that right. Clearly, I've been hanging around vampires for too long!'

The wheels skidded to a stop and the great doors to the Lazar family home swung wide. The twins' grandparents bustled out to the drive, looking majestic even though it was only 7 o'clock in the morning, Transylvania time! The Countess wore a silk skirt of jade green paired with a satin off-the-shoulder top, while the Count greeted them in a fancy, ruffled chemise that blossomed out from the front of his charcoal coat.

'Welcome! Welcome!' cried the Count, striding down the steps.

Seeing them – even so soon after their visit to Franklin Grove – chased the jet lag straight out of Olivia. At least for now. The girls rushed over to their grandparents, Olivia's camera dangling around her neck. She managed to push it aside right before the Countess wrapped her in a tight hug.

Lillian curtseyed politely. 'Nice to see you again, sir.'

Olivia's grandfather tilted his head, looking at her standing there so formally, before pulling her into a warm embrace. 'Welcome to our home, Lillian!'

Lillian's eyes bugged over the Count's shoulder

before her lips parted in a wide smile. 'Thank you,' she stammered and Olivia's heart warmed. The moment was so sweet she wished she could save it and put it on a greeting card.

Meanwhile, Horatio didn't waste a single second. Now that he was back on the job, he rushed around the family, collecting everyone's luggage. 'I will have these inside and up to your rooms in just a moment. And don't worry, Count and Countess Lazar, as soon as I have finished attending to the bags, I will be at your service. I imagine there is a great deal of work awaiting me. I have been away for *far* too long.'

'Absolutely not,' said the Countess, raising one eyebrow at her butler. 'You may not go back to work after having just returned home on an overnight flight, Horatio.'

'But, Madam, I must –'

The Countess lifted her chin. 'Not another word. I insist you take the day off. You need your rest. We have a big weekend ahead, after all.'

Horatio's shoulders slumped. Olivia had never known anyone to be so against having a *holiday*.

'Here, Horatio.' Charles scooped up two of the bags, one in each hand. 'Let me help you with these. I'm sure all your work will still be waiting for you tomorrow morning.' With that, the adults made their way up to the house.

Olivia heard a familiar voice from inside the house: 'Is that the Vegas I hear?' Excitement bubbled up inside her. Prince Alex emerged in the doorway. 'It *is*!' He looked utterly royal in his tailored trousers and midnight-blue button-down shirt, but that was nothing compared to the girl beside him.

Ivy drew a sharp breath and Olivia knew exactly why. Their new friend Tessa waved from the mansion, as graceful as a movie star. There was no sign that she had ever been a serving girl. Olivia remembered when Tessa had been so shy that she'd nearly blended into the tapestries. But now, her eyes were bright and open and her mouth was curved into a soft smile. Her porcelain skin seemed to be lit from the inside. She was dazzling.

'Wow, she's beautiful,' breathed Olivia. *And so happy with Alex*, she added in her head. Olivia was suddenly very glad that the saying 'green with envy' was only that – a saying – or else she was sure her face would have an olive tinge.

Tessa practically floated down the stairs. She reached out and grasped both girls' hands. 'I'm so glad to see you both. I was worried that since the wedding was so far away, you might not be able to make it, but here you are!' She squeezed. 'And Olivia, I saw your performance in *The Groves*. You were magnificent.'

'Oh!' exclaimed Olivia, startled by the mention of the movie. 'Thank you, but,' she said, quickly trying to shift subjects, 'I'm much more excited about the wedding!'

Tessa pressed her hands to her heart. 'Me too! And I'm so thrilled it's going to be *here*!' She glanced back, admiring the Lazar mansion.

'Here?' Olivia and Ivy asked in unison.

'Er . . . not that we're not pleased, too,' said Ivy, 'but why aren't you having the wedding at the royal palace?'

Alex stepped forwards, putting his arm around Tessa's slight shoulders. 'Your grandparents' manor is among the most romantic in all of Europe. It is said that, long ago, it was the scene of many romantic proposals and declarations of undying love, because this is where the Free Rose of Summer blooms.'

Ivy tilted her head. 'I don't think I've ever heard of that tradition and I'm a vamp, so I *know* my sister hasn't.'

Olivia stuck out her tongue at Ivy.

Alex chuckled. 'Then we will have to show you. I'm due to visit Wallachia Academy later today to go over some last-minute wedding plans with the school head, who is to be a witness at the wedding. But I should just have time . . . Come with me.' He beckoned, and Olivia and Ivy followed him and Tessa across the lush grounds towards the back of the mansion.

On the other side was a beautiful green field. The group walked up to the crest of a hill that overlooked the blossoming Lazar garden with its colourful violets, tulips and lilies. Vampires, with their advanced horticultural skills, certainly did have green fingers!

Alex took Tessa's hand and pointed down to the other side of the hill, where the land flattened into a blooming rose meadow. Olivia had never seen anything like it before. The garden was planted with beds of red, pink, yellow, peach, lavender, blue, purple and white. A huge greenhouse –

bigger than Ivy's home back in Franklin Grove – nestled on the edge of the meadow.

'It's fabulous,' said Olivia, taking a deep breath of the fragrant air.

'Like all flowers,' said Alex, 'these roses can live for years and years when aided by vampire cultivation techniques. But despite how strong and long-living these flowers are, at the very height of summer a fierce breeze blows through the grounds, plucking a single rose from the meadow and stealing it away. It happens every year.'

Olivia tried to imagine what that would look like, a single flower soaring through the air.

'Of course,' Alex went on, 'no one has actually *seen* this occur for a long, long time, but it is said that the colour of the rose holds significance for any who witness it. For example, yellow means "new beginnings", while lavender means "enchantment".'

'Almost all colours promise good fortune,'

added Tessa. 'Except blue, which means "impossible love".'

'Impossible love does not exist,' said Alex, sharing a meaningful look with Tessa. Even though their love had seemed impossible, it had worked out. Ivy and Olivia had convinced Tessa at the Valentine's Ball this year that she could be with Alex and still stay true to herself. Together, she and Alex had overcome the odds and now they were getting married! Maybe Alex was right and no love *was* impossible.

But I *know that's not exactly true*, Olivia thought, with a rueful pout. She forced her lips into a smile and hoped no one noticed.

Tessa rested her head on Alex's shoulder. 'I want our whole wedding day to be filled with flowers.' Olivia sighed but didn't speak, letting them enjoy their moment. Ivy rolled her eyes.

In silence, they all looked out at the rose meadow. It was hard not to feel a little starry-eyed with the combination of the view and Alex's romantic superstition. Olivia's breath had literally been taken away. She'd had no idea her family's land was the site of such a beautiful and romantic legend.

'Um, guys?' Ivy stepped forwards, peering down the hill. 'Isn't this the hill I fell down last time we were here?'

Olivia burst out laughing. Leave it to her sister to puncture such a tender moment!

'Well, with that parting thought . . .' Alex's eyes sparkled '. . . we should probably be heading back to the house. There's a lot to do before the big day!' He and Tessa exchanged a loving smile, and Olivia found herself having to suppress another wistful sigh.

'He's right,' Tessa agreed. 'And we've stolen you from your grandparents for too long already. But, you two have to promise to come to my *O Inima Sarbatoare*.'

'Oh Enemy Sar Batter?' Olivia tried to repeat the words.

Tessa chuckled. '*O Inima Sarbatoare*,' she said the words slowly.

'Oh In-ee-ma Sar-bat-or,' Ivy echoed in a very American accent.

'Tessa?' Olivia interrupted. 'I think our Romanian might be a little rusty. It sounds like you're speaking jibberish!'

Tessa frowned. 'I'm sorry. It doesn't have an English translation that I know. Its literal meaning is "One Heart Celebration".'

'One Heart Celebration?' Ivy repeated. 'No offence, but that sounds sort of sad.'

Tessa smiled. 'It's traditionally held two nights before a wedding to mark that a person has just one more night as a lonely heart.' She intertwined her fingers in Alex's. 'Because after that, I'll forever be part of a pair.' Olivia didn't dare look at Ivy, who was surely approaching her tolerance level for mushy love stuff.

Olivia kept one eye on the rose meadow, half hoping she would spot the Free Rose. 'In America, we call that a bachelorette party.' Olivia tried to picture Tessa running around in a silly veil made of toilet paper and singing bad karaoke, like at the bachelorette parties she'd seen on TV shows back home. 'But . . . I have a feeling that the Transylvanian vampire version will be a *much* classier affair.'

'But don't think you girls are having all the fun.' Prince Alex waggled his eyebrows. 'I'm having my own One Heart Celebration. It's just a shame Brendan and –' The whole world seemed to lurch into slow motion for Olivia. *He's going to say it, isn't he? The J-word.* He was going to say the J-word and there was nothing she could do to stop him. She could see Alex's mouth forming the word. She could make out Ivy's shadow, stretching out in front of her, arms waving like she was trying to stop a car crash. Then Tessa was reaching for Alex, but before she could grab him, he finished, '– Jackson couldn't be here.'

Ivy's jaw dropped and Tessa stopped dead. Olivia suddenly felt as if all the oxygen in the entire world had been sucked up by the sky.

Alex's eyes flitted between the faces staring at him. 'Um . . . I mean . . .' he stuttered. 'You know, I just thought . . .' Tessa gently touched her fiancé's arm. 'My apologies.' He bowed his head to Olivia.

Olivia swished her hand and did her best to curve her lips into a bright smile. 'Don't worry about it.' To avoid eye contact, Olivia made a show of glancing around. 'Hey, if you guys are heading back now, I think I'll catch up with you in a minute. I want to practise my photography a little before the wedding.'

Ivy squeezed Olivia's arm. 'You totally should! Look at this meadow. Your shots are going to be awesome.'

Olivia breathed a sigh of relief. Ivy knew exactly when her twin was looking for an exit strategy. *Super sister to the rescue!*

As Tessa and Alex turned to walk back towards the mansion, Ivy murmured, 'Are you sure you'll be OK?'

'I'm fine!' Olivia insisted. She was starting to sound like a broken record.

'All right, then.' Ivy shrugged. 'I guess I'll see you back at the castle.' She trotted after Prince Alex and Tessa, who were walking at least two feet apart. Even though she felt a pang of sadness, Olivia was quite touched by their effort to avoid rubbing their couple-ness in her face. Then she frowned. It was their wedding weekend, though, and she hoped they wouldn't allow her situation to get in the way of what should be the most romantic time of their lives. Olivia shook herself. She really needed to pull herself out of this funk before she became a walking, talking mood-killer!

She made her way down the opposite side of the hill and crouched in the long grass. Focusing the lens, she pointed her camera at the roses. The early-morning Transylvanian sun washed the flowers with a warm glow – the view could have been straight out of a postcard. Olivia enjoyed the *click-click-click* of her snapping camera. She could get lost in the scenery and in capturing the perfect shot. It was such a relief! Birds trilled and squawked as the wind ruffled the grass.

Olivia brought her lens round to the massive greenhouse with its clear glass walls. Sunshine flashed off the surface. Horatio must have needed truckloads of Spray 'n' Shine to keep it that pristine. Inside, an older woman – probably a vampire judging by her paleness – was potting up flower bulbs. She wore a dark-green apron and canvas gloves, and her frizzy grey hair was pulled back in a messy ponytail.

Something moved at the edge of the greenhouse. Olivia squinted. There was a tall figure lurking near the far wall. She peered through her camera, zooming in. Horatio came into focus, a forlorn look on his face as he stared through the glass at the gardener. *Oh my goodness!* Olivia had to stop herself from squealing. The puppy-dog eyes, the waiting around with his hands in his pockets – *does Horatio have a crush?*

Olivia was wondering whether she should go over and talk to him. She didn't exactly feel right squatting here spying on the butler. But suddenly she was slapped in the face by her own hair. She froze, her heart thudding in her chest. Alex's story echoed in her head: . . . *a fierce breeze will blow through the grounds, plucking a single rose from the meadow and stealing it away* . . . Was she about to see the Free Rose?

But as Olivia turned to stare back at the

meadow, the wind slowly died. There was no floating rose-head. *Which means*, she thought, *I still have no idea what the future holds . . .*

Chapter Four

'Do you think you need a passport to visit the other end of this table?' Ivy whispered to her sister. She was seated with Olivia near the end of the Lazar's ridiculously long dining table. Sparkling chandeliers dripped crystal overhead, and white marble columns stretched to the ceiling. The table was covered with an ornate crimson cloth embroidered in gold, on top of which rows of candles flickered and cast a warm glow.

Olivia almost choked on her water and Ivy patted her back, giggling. The twins, along with a dozen other vampires, were waiting to begin

Tessa's One Heart Celebration, but the princess-to-be was already fifteen minutes late. The wait wouldn't have been so bad if there had been even a morsel of food on the table, but until the guest of honour herself arrived no festivities could begin, and that meant the servers would not bring out any food. Ivy's mouth watered at the thought of mounds of buttered rolls and decadent chocolate-amaretto cake. The Lazars employed only the top graduates from the Transylvanian School of Culinary Arts, which meant they employed the best young vampire chefs in the whole world.

'I hope everything's all right,' said Olivia once she'd recovered. She was watching the door for any sign of Tessa's arrival. The other guests, frankly, seemed unconcerned. Around the table sat several other vamp girls, each with perfectly straightened hair and movie-set makeovers. 'She's going to miss her own you-know-what ceremony.'

Ivy rolled her eyes.

'What?' Olivia rested her fists on her hips. She was wearing a hot-pink halter dress and a long strand of pearls that clinked together every time she moved. 'You have to admit it's an awful name for a ceremony. We have to come up with a better English translation. Lucky Heart . . . Happy Heart . . . Bride-to-be Bash . . . I don't know! Seriously, though, where *is* she?' Olivia turned in her chair, checking the room, as if Tessa might have snuck in without anyone noticing.

Ivy glanced again at her watch. 'Calm down, Miss I-Take-Two-Hours-To-Get-Ready. I'm sure she'll be here any minute.'

'I do *not*!' Olivia gently swatted her sister then returned to twiddling her thumbs in her lap. Ivy was feeling restless too. She could practically feel the vamp girls judging her as they shot her looks in between twirling shiny strands of hair around their manicured talons. She hoped Tessa really would be there any minute. *Nothing could have gone wrong, could it?*

Olivia leaned over. 'Do you think we should try to get some work done while we wait? Georgia would flip if she thought that we were slacking on such an important magazine assignment. Maybe we could get a few sound bites from the others?'

Ivy fiddled with the notepad in her lap. Their fellow guests were so standoffish and aloof. They were wearing sunglasses, despite the fact that the Banquet Hall was dim and candle-lit. They were so snooty they made Franklin Grove's resident diva, Charlotte Brown, look down-to-earth! Ivy shuddered. Even Olivia – who gave everyone the benefit of the doubt – was starting to look unimpressed by the unwelcoming behaviour of the vampire girls.

'Do we have to?' Ivy muttered. One of the vampire's heads snapped up and Ivy winced. She had spent so much time with humans back in Franklin Grove that she'd forgotten everyone here would have super vamp hearing. She tried to give an apologetic smile but the girl flipped her hair and turned away.

Was this 'polite' vampire society? And, worse, did these girls go to school at Wallachia Academy? Ivy cleared her throat, suddenly determined. They might not be the best interviewees in the world, but she had a job to do and was determined to be a professional for her first real reporting gig.

'Excuse me.' She craned round to smile at the vampire nearest her, opening her notepad to a blank page. If it weren't for the diamond-encrusted sunglasses, the girl would have looked totally goth gorgeous in her blood-red evening dress and tasteful silver necklace. 'I'm Ivy Vega and I was wondering if you might be kind enough to answer a few questions for me. See, I'm writing an article for *VAMP* magazine and my sister and I are covering the entire Vampire

Royal Wedding. Would you mind?'

The girl shrugged and coolly lifted her perfectly arched eyebrows. 'If you must.'

'Great!' Ivy's voice came out squeaky. She noticed the heads of the other vampires tilt in the direction of the conversation, but they all pretended not to listen. *They really should drop the unfriendly act*, Ivy thought. *It doesn't look good on them.* 'Right,' she started. 'Firstly, what's your name?'

'Ivana. Pleased to meet you.' She extended her fingers. Ivy awkwardly grasped Ivana's fingers and gave them a little shake.

The vamp next to her, dressed in a sequined cocktail dress, gasped as if Ivy had made a huge faux-pas.

'Pleasure,' said Ivy as Ivana wiped her hand on her dress. 'How long have you been friends with Tessa?' She uncapped her pen.

'We've never met,' Ivana drawled in a husky voice.

Ivy bit her lip, furrowing her eyebrows. 'I'm not sure I understand. If you're not friends, why are you here?'

'Isn't it obvious?' Ivana twirled a strand of hair around her finger. 'Because Tessa will one day be queen, of course. It's a good idea to *become* her friend, no?'

Ivy shot Olivia a covert glance and she could tell her sister was thinking the same thing – *yuck!* How many of the other guests didn't know Tessa at all? Surely they weren't all just a bunch of social climbers?

'Um, well, thanks for that.' She closed her notepad. 'That was really . . . fascinating.'

Ivy nudged Olivia and gestured to the vampire nearest her. Olivia took one look at the girl, who was busy studying her manicure, and turned back to Ivy.

No way, she mouthed, eyes wide.

The vamp girl was tall and a bit of a Glamazon.

OK, so she was actually quite scary. Ivy nodded at Olivia, as if to say she understood her sister's hesitation.

Then Ivy gave Olivia a harder nudge, so that she bumped into the Glamazon girl.

'Sorry!' Olivia yelped and shot Ivy a deadly glare.

'Oops!' Ivy batted her eyelashes and prepared to take notes.

The Glamazon looked at Olivia like she was a piece of gum stuck to the bottom of her stiletto.

'Hi!' Olivia waved, even though she was right under the vamp girl's nose. 'I'm Olivia. How are you and, um –' she wiggled herself back on to her own chair – 'how do you know Tessa?'

The Glamazon scooted her chair back a little. 'My name is Arabella, and who is this Tessa person that you speak of? I've never heard of her.'

Ivy knew it was bad manners, but she couldn't help it. She put her elbows on the table and leaned across Olivia. 'Tessa . . . the girl who is going to marry Prince Alex . . . Any of this ring a bell?'

Arabella shrugged and turned her face away. 'Not really.'

Ivy flipped her notepad shut. Getting appropriate sound bites here was not going to be easy. *I wonder if* VAMP *magazine would like a feature on the impossible levels of snootiness among posh vampires? Because I could write a whole book about that!*

The Banquet Hall doors swung open and Horatio stepped out, looking dapper in a sleek black tuxedo. 'Announcing the arrival of Petra Tarasov, Anastasia Gorya, Nastya Petrov and Kristina Kazimir.' *More vampires? Oh great – the snootiness factor has just gone up by fifty per cent.*

But, maybe not – these girls were sporting evening wear that was a little less rigid and much more vintage. Plus, they weren't wearing sunglasses. Even better – they were actually *smiling.*

'Hi, girls!' One of the new guests pulled out a chair and plopped down between Ivy and Olivia.

'I'm Petra.' She wore a black shift with a funky lace hem. 'So sorry we're late.' Ivy caught traces of various European accents – totally different to the Transylvanian one shared by the girls who had stonewalled her. 'We had this assembly at the Academy that ran a little late. You know what a bore teachers can be.' Her eyes flicked to the ceiling. 'I'm sure we're all capable of waiting until Monday to hear our millionth lecture on the importance of eating a balanced red-blood-cell diet.'

Ivy felt as if a fist had clenched around her stomach. *Did she say 'the Academy'? As in 'Wallachia Academy'?* Ivy sat up straighter. This was going to be her first glimpse of the kind of people she might, maybe, *possibly* be studying with, and they seemed much cooler than the snooty Snobzillas who had been cold-shouldering her and Olivia so far tonight.

'Hey!' Petra's eyes lit up. 'You ladies are the

American twins writing that *VAMP* magazine article, aren't you? I have to talk to you two later.' Her tone was hushed and excited, like she was asking Ivy to share a particularly juicy piece of gossip. 'I want to know everything about America. Like why do you call those yummy potato things "French fries"?'

Ivy and Olivia laughed for the first time that evening. Maybe this party wouldn't be a total flop after all.

Petra looked around. 'Where is Tessa, anyway?' she asked the other guests at the table, but nobody bothered to answer. The new girls' presence had done nothing to thaw their ice-queen acts.

'We're not sure,' Olivia chimed in, shifting in her seat. 'I'm starting to get worr–'

'I'm here! I'm here!' Tessa rushed into the Banquet Hall before Horatio could properly announce her arrival. She skidded to a stop at the head of the dining table where the snooty vamp girls were staring open-mouthed.

She looked beautiful, but a little ragged. Her navy-blue dress hung unevenly and her up-do wasn't as sleek as it could be. *Whoa*, thought Ivy, *where did that come from? Since when was I a serving member of the Fashion Police?* Clearly, Olivia had been rubbing off on her.

'I'm late. Oh goodness, I know, I'm so late.' Tessa smoothed her hair, tucking a hairgrip back into place.

Horatio nodded to the waiting servants and they swooped in with shiny platters of bite-sized appetisers: blood-sausage links wrapped in crescent rolls; miniature slivers of toast with pâté; and small vials of blood smoothie.

Tessa stood apart from the group and looked like she didn't know how to proceed. Gone were the confidence and movie-star poise Ivy had seen earlier that day. In fact, she looked like the same shy serving girl Ivy had first met. She should have been commanding the room, not cowering in it. After all, it wouldn't be long until she was *Princess* Tessa.

All eyes were on the bride-to-be, the silence more awkward than any Ivy had ever experienced. Tessa parted her lips and then seemed to think better of saying anything more. She even looked uncertain about whether or not she should take a seat!

'Perhaps we should kick things off with a game,' suggested Petra.

'Great idea!' Olivia clapped.

Ivy grinned to herself – not just at the sight of her twin's excitement about party games, but because it was a Wallachia girl who had come to the rescue! She was starting to warm to Petra already. Maybe the famous school was not going to be full of stuck-up vamp girls, after all.

'How about Secrets and Lies?' A sly smile formed on Petra's lips.

'What's that?' asked Ivy and Olivia at the same time. They immediately both cringed. It was a little too creepily twin-tastic when they did the whole talk-in-unison thing. 'Sorry,' they both said. *Not again!*

Petra just giggled. 'It's this cool vampire game where one person is asked a series of very direct, very personal questions.' She drummed her fingertips together mischievously. 'And the person being asked is supposed to tell the truth. It's almost impossible to lie, since vampire sensitivity and super-hearing make us experts at knowing when people are lying. We can catch all the giveaways like subtleties in voice, tone – even the most minor change in heartbeat. One teensy untruth and we'll call the liar out!'

Ivy glanced nervously at Olivia. She didn't want her to feel left out since she was the only non-vampire in the room, but Olivia was leaning in, her elbows propped on the table. 'Really?' she asked excitedly. 'You can tell just from listening to people talk?'

'Sure can,' said Petra, lifting her chin.

'You know, you guys would make killer spies!' Olivia's eyes were wide.

'The game?' reminded Ivy before Olivia went too far off-track.

'Right,' said Petra. 'Maybe Tessa can start, since it's her ceremony and all.'

Tessa backed away, waving her hands in front of her. 'No, that's all right. Actually, I have to excuse myself. One moment.' She held up a finger and Ivy noticed not only the sparkly engagement ring, but the way Tessa was trembling. 'I'll be right back.'

Ivy watched her leave the room, her navy gown swirling behind her. Something was definitely up with Tessa, but what could it be?

Ivana shook her head slowly. 'Tsk, tsk. How rude. And *she's* supposed to be a *princess*?'

She jutted her chin and stared down her nose. 'But that's probably just an indication of her upbringing.'

Arabella the Glamazon murmured her agreement.

Ivy opened her mouth to speak, but Petra beat her to it. 'Sorry, Ivana. Let me get this straight. *You* think *Tessa* is rude? Not so long ago she would have been waiting on the people in this room and now she's supposed to be sitting at the head of the table. Of course she's going to be nervous. And people like you judging her upbringing isn't going to help. Give her a break.' Petra leaned back in her chair, folding her arms.

Ivy caught Petra's eye and smiled. At least someone in this social circle was a little less uptight.

Chapter Five

Is it morning already?

Shards of light shot through the blinds like laser beams on to Olivia's face. She buried her head in the crook of her arm, still sleepy. Maybe she wasn't cut out to be a jet-setter. These changes in time zone were killing her!

Just as she was about to roll out of bed, Olivia stopped herself, feet dangling in mid air. In her exhausted state she had completely forgotten that she was on the top bunk of the custom-made bunk bed-and-coffin in their Transylvania bed chamber. She was *so* not in Franklin Grove any more.

This time, more carefully, Olivia slid her toes to where she could rest them on Ivy's closed coffin lid and stepped softly down. Their grandparents had imported a top-of-the-line Interna-3 coffin just like Ivy used at home. They really did want the girls to feel comfortable in Transylvania.

Olivia rapped her knuckles on Ivy's vampy version of a bed. 'Hello? Anybody home?' She cracked open the lid, but there was no Ivy. Was her sister up and about already? That was strange; Ivy loathed mornings. She always claimed to be allergic to 'Before 9 a.m.'.

Olivia pulled on a denim skirt and a pale-pink V-neck. With any luck, Horatio would have a giant stack of pancakes ready and waiting. But just as her mouth was starting to water at the thought of melted butter and rich maple syrup, Olivia noticed the flickering yellow light of the desktop computer.

Ivy had left it in sleep mode.

She chewed her lip. It would be so easy to log on to the internet and check her emails. It would only take two minutes, tops. What could it hurt? Perhaps Jackson had sent her a message? *I know we promised not to get in touch but . . .* She couldn't ignore the niggling ache in her heart whenever she imagined not speaking to him again. *Who knew that love and romance would turn out to be so painful?* Perhaps he'd been struggling too. After all, he found time to blog – wouldn't he even be tempted to send her a message whilst he was on the computer? Or would it just make her all the more unhappy to find her inbox empty?

That settled it. She shoved a tube of lipgloss in her pocket and marched to the door. It was time to quit obsessing. *I have a life, you know!* But at the doorway she stopped short, a worm of curiosity wiggling into her brain. *OK, maybe for just a couple of minutes . . . max.*

Olivia sat down and tapped the keyboard,

lighting up the screen. She held her breath as she logged on to her email. Her inbox popped up. There was an email from Camilla, one from Sophia and even one from her classmate Jenny, asking if she had any decorating tips for her cousin's birthday party.

But there was nothing from Jackson.

She checked her junk mail – just in case. Still nothing. Her heart slid all the way down to her pink-varnished toes.

Olivia drummed her fingertips on the desk. *No biggie.* He had been practically living on movie sets. What could she expect? Olivia knew what making films was like – she knew it was crazily busy and that Jackson was probably not getting a moment to himself. *It's not like I need him to check in every ten seconds, right?*

Olivia typed the web address to *Jackson's Journal*, the online blog he kept as a continuation of his bestselling book from earlier that year.

He had probably only had time to jot a couple of lines of updates: *Such-and-such city is great! The movie's good! I'm too exhausted to move!*

The page loaded and, instead, Olivia was greeted with high-res photos of European landmarks. And not just any landmarks – *romantic* landmarks. There he was at the Eiffel Tower; and here he was lounging in the grass in front of the Leaning Tower of Pisa. He must have been taking a trip around Europe. Below each picture, he'd written long passages of text describing the sights and his thoughts about them.

Bonjour from the Tour d'Eiffel! Here I am in the City of Light and Love and may I just say: I'm totally digging it! Nicknamed the 'Iron Lady', the Eiffel Tower is even cooler up close than it is in pictures . . .

Olivia's jaw dropped. These blog posts had *obviously* taken a long time to put together – but he couldn't come up with a few minutes to write her one measly email! She felt her chest throb.

She shook herself. Where were these feelings coming from? And why was it that she almost didn't want him to have a good time? She knew it was silly, but she'd somehow feel better if she knew he was missing her at least a little. *But noooo* . . . She did a mental eye-roll. *He's off being Mr Big Movie Star and probably can't even remember if I spell my last name with one 'b' or two.*

She punched the power button and the screen went black. '*I* can be busy as well, *Jackson*,' Olivia said as the tears began to well up in her eyes and clog her throat. She shoved back from the desk and marched to the door, pulling it open and colliding with Charles, who was passing on the landing. She stumbled backwards, starting to fall, but Charles snatched out a hand with vampire quickness to stop her.

'That was a close one,' he said, patting her shoulder.

'It was a little painful.' Olivia rubbed her

forehead whilst trying to smile. Bumping into a vampire was like walking into a brick wall.

Charles chuckled. 'My apologies, Olivia.'

She felt her head. She didn't want a big, fat bump messing up the hair style she had planned for the wedding. 'Do you know where Ivy's gone?'

Charles adjusted his thin red tie and brushed the lapel of his navy blazer. 'She's out with your grandmother this morning.' Olivia didn't need to be told any more. It had to be Wallachia stuff – one more thing to give her a sick feeling in the pit of her stomach.

It was starting to feel . . . *real.* Ivy might not be coming back to Franklin Grove with her. First Jackson and now her twin. It seemed like *everyone* was leaving her.

'You're welcome to join Lillian and me for breakfast out on the terrace,' her bio-dad offered.

Olivia rubbed her temples, trying to erase the sad thoughts. 'Thanks, but I think I'm going to skip breakfast and get some work done while Ivy's away.'

Charles frowned. 'It's first thing in the morning. What is there to be done for your article?'

Olivia laughed at his bewilderment. 'There is a wedding happening *tomorrow* in *this* house. And that means that somewhere in this ginormous mansion, there is some craziness happening; some task that needs some organising.'

Charles looked thoughtful. 'You're right. Weddings can take a lot of organising. The outfits, the wedding favours, the music for the first dance . . .'

Olivia shook her head. *Since when has he been thinking about all this sort of stuff?*

'Here we are.' Ivy's grandmother kissed her cheek. 'I will leave you to it. This decision has to be yours and yours alone. I don't want you to feel as if I'm hovering over you, pressuring you one way or the other.' She peered at Ivy from underneath an elegant, wide-brimmed hat.

Ivy gazed up at the towering iron gates of Wallachia Academy. The Countess had crept into Ivy's room early that morning and rapped on her coffin. Apparently her grandmother didn't know about her strict policy against activities pre-9 a.m. After Ivy had bolted down a quick breakfast of plasma pancakes, Horatio had driven the two of them here. Now she was completely overwhelmed by the spindly turrets and stone gargoyles of the old, Gothic buildings.

Large bats and a thorny rose-stem design were carved into the wrought-iron gates, supported by two massive pillars. In the middle was the same crest Ivy had been obsessing over every day on her computer – two bats on either side of a blood-red shield. Ivy felt like she was dreaming. After imagining it and thinking about it almost constantly, here she was, actually *at* Wallachia.

Should I go or should I not? That had been the persistent question on Ivy's mind, and this visit was the biggest step yet towards making that decision.

Ivy squeezed her grandmother's hand. 'I'll see you soon,' she said. 'And I promise to give it a fair chance.'

The Countess smiled. 'That's all I ask.'

The gates creaked as they were dragged open by a tall, spooky vampire in a dark-grey suit, who looked like he might have been related to Horatio. *Here goes nothing.* Ivy waved one last goodbye to the Countess and Horatio – who showed no sign of recognising the spooky vampire – before stepping inside. The campus was quiet and peaceful, like a fancy cemetery without the headstones. Pristine emerald lawns stretched as far as she could see, and neatly raked gravel crunched beneath her feet on the drive. Flags bearing the school motif fluttered from the towers and the mullioned windows winked in the sunlight. *This place makes Franklin Grove look cheap and nasty!* she thought, remembering how impressed Olivia had been when she'd first seen the school's ivy-covered pillars back at home. Wallachia Academy was off the scale.

Ivy suddenly felt very self-conscious in her jeans and black T-shirt. *Perhaps I should have gone with my wrap dress, after all . . .*

'Welcome to Wallachia Academy, Miss Vega,' said Horatio Two. 'I trust you will enjoy your visit.' *If only Olivia were here! She would have been super-scared of the old-school vamp.* Ivy felt a stab of sorrow. This was an area of her life that Olivia would never be able to be a part of.

Ivy forced the thought out of her mind. She had promised her grandmother she would put her best foot forward. Forcing an Olivia-style smile on her face, she continued up the impossibly long and curving walkway that led to the main building.

'Wallachia Academy was founded by Vladimir Ivanov, the longest-living vampire of all time.' Horatio Two trailed one step behind her, reciting the school's history. They passed a large stone sculpture of a stern-looking vampire riding a stately-looking horse. 'The Academy,' he continued, 'has produced some of the finest vampire thespians, artists and Nobel laureates. In fact, it was right here under this very stone archway that Shakespeare wrote his first sonnet.'

'Shakespeare was a vampire?' Ivy spluttered.

Horatio Two leaned in and lowered his voice. 'In an early draft of *Romeo and Juliet*, the Montagues were based on a very well-regarded family here in Transylvania.' *Woah! Just wait until I tell Sophia*, Ivy thought. *She'll be amazed!* Then Ivy's heart sank a little bit – she had no idea when she'd be seeing her friend next. Ivy felt cast adrift without her old friends, and so far she had no new friends at all.

The sound of their footsteps echoed on the

black-and-white marble floors as Horatio Two led Ivy inside to a cavernous reception area.

'You may have a seat, Miss Vega.' He gestured to a row of what Ivy could only describe as thrones. At least, they were the plushest chairs she had ever seen in a waiting room. 'Your guide will be with you shortly.'

Ivy climbed on to one of the red velvet chairs, feet dangling awkwardly. The room was deadly silent and Ivy took the opportunity to look around. A sparkling chandelier hung from the ceiling and a full-sized coat of armour stood guarding the doorway. Ivy felt very small and – worse – she realised she was slouching in the swanky chair. *One does not slouch one's body in such elegant surroundings!* Ivy thought, practising her best Wallachia-appropriate way of talking. She sat up straight, tapping her fingers on the chair's slick mahogany arm, then went back to slouching. She would sit how she liked – fancy room or not! Ivy sighed, shaking her head. Maybe she was overreacting. She had almost started an argument . . . with herself . . . in an empty room . . .

Talk about over-thinking things!

But she was still confused about the entire situation. She wanted to know more about her vampire self, but she definitely didn't want to have the 'Ivy' beaten out of her.

'I heard you were visiting today.' Ivy jumped in her seat, turning to the door in time to see Petra slinking inside.

Instantly, Ivy felt better – more positive. 'Are you going to be my guide?'

Petra wore a pristine, classical-style school uniform, one that Ivy was *not* looking forward to wearing. The whole red pleated skirt and knee-high sock thing was so not her style. Petra grinned wickedly. 'I will be . . . in a minute.'

Just then, a receptionist with a tight bun and

shiny black shoes clacked into the waiting room carrying a clipboard. 'Ivy Vega?' she asked.

Before Ivy could respond, Petra was skipping her way over to the woman. 'Miss Dina,' she said sweetly. 'Excuse me, but there's been a slight change of plan.' She reached over and pointed to a spot on Miss Dina's clipboard. 'Ursula can't make it and she asked me to take today's tour. Is that all right?'

Ivy held her breath. She realised from the way Petra grinned a moment ago that her new friend was probably lying. But Miss Dina just scribbled something on her clipboard and said, 'Very well. Make sure to have Miss Vega back on time, please.' *If lying were a sport, Petra would be a professional! She managed to get one past an adult vamp!*

Petra winked at Ivy. 'Follow me,' she said, beckoning with one finger. Ivy sprang out of the chair and followed Petra through the great double doors and out into an arching hallway with flickering lanterns.

Maybe this place *wouldn't* beat the 'Ivy' out of her. Petra still seemed to have plenty of personality. Even if a part of that personality happened to be a talent for telling lies.

Olivia leaned against the massive doorway of the Great Hall in the Lazars' home. She remembered the Valentine's Ball from earlier in the year. The hall had been decorated with deep red roses and candles that cast a romantic glow throughout the room, but the most memorable part of the evening had been when her bio-dad had been reconciled with his parents after years of not speaking. Tomorrow, it would be the scene of the wedding of Prince Alex and soon-to-be-Princess Tessa. Olivia tried to imagine what it would look like once all the preparations were finished.

She nervously inched inside, watching the

servants arrange the rows of chairs and polish the huge black vases that lined the aisle, waiting to be filled with flowers.

A statuesque woman stood in the centre of it all, waving her hands like a conductor. 'No, not there!' she directed. 'Move it over five centimetres; five centimetres precisely.' She pointed to one of the vases. 'No, not like that. Oh, here, let me do it.' The terrified servant scurried out of her way.

She must be the wedding planner, thought Olivia. *But she's dressed like she's going to a funeral.* Olivia studied the vampire's tailored black suit. *A very* expensive *funeral!*

Suddenly, the woman span around. 'You!' She singled out Olivia. 'Are you with the caterer?' Olivia straightened, shaking her head. 'No? Then what are you doing here?'

'Um . . .' She held up the camera she was carrying around her neck. 'I'm the guest photographer for *VAMP* magazine and, well, my sister and I are doing a big feature on the vampire royal wedding. I wondered if I could take some photos. We want to chronicle the massive effort everyone's putting into getting things ready for the big day.' Before the wedding planner could protest, Olivia added, 'Oh, and I totally agree. The vase looks better there. You have a great eye!'

The corners of the woman's mouth twitched. 'I guess I don't see why not – as long as you keep out of the way.'

'Great!' Olivia said. 'You won't even know I'm here. I promise.' She stepped back, but in doing so nearly tipped over a vase. Olivia gasped, managing to steady it just in time. The woman lifted an eyebrow. 'Starting now!' Olivia squeaked, feeling her shoulders hunch up to her ears. She retreated slowly to an unpopulated corner of the hall.

The wedding planner huffed, saying something to a servant nearby. *OK, lady,* Olivia thought, *I might not have vampire super-hearing, but I'm not blind!*

An older woman with frizzy grey hair approached the wedding planner, toting a large wicker basket. Olivia recognised her from the big greenhouse yesterday – it was Horatio's crush! And she had quite the green thumb, it seemed. Olivia marvelled at the flowers overflowing from the basket. The woman had grown some extra special ones for the occasion, it seemed. Olivia held the viewfinder up to her eye and zoomed in for a better look. They truly were spectacular, so much so that she didn't even recognise the different types of flowers. She stared at the purple, magenta, cream and aqua hues. They weren't like roses or daffodils or lilies. They weren't like anything she had ever seen. Not that Olivia was surprised. With all those hundreds of years' practice, vampires were advanced at practically everything they did – even horticulture!

The wedding planner pinched a stem between

two fingers and twirled it in front of her nose. 'No.' She tossed that one over her shoulder and selected a different flower. 'No.' A flurry of petals, like a rainbow storm, fell on to the floor. 'No, no, no! Too much colour!' she screamed, accidentally stomping on a gorgeous amethyst bloom. 'These are entirely wrong! Don't come back until you have something suitable.' She shooed the gardener away and Olivia felt her eyes grow wide. She must really be out-of-touch with vampire fashion because she thought those flowers had been absolutely stunning! The gardener lifted her chin, snatched back her basket and strode off. Olivia felt bad for her – she could bet it took *months* to cultivate such perfect blooms.

'Excuse me, Madam?' A servant girl in a white frock tapped the wedding planner's arm. 'Where will the band be positioned? We would like to clear a space.'

The wedding planner tugged at the ends of

her hair. 'Band? There will be no band!' She rested her forehead in her palm and shook her head vigorously. When she resurfaced, her face was so pink it looked as if she'd run a mile. 'There will be exactly one pianist – there – in the corner.' Olivia was relieved when the woman didn't single out *her* corner. 'Simple and direct.' The wedding planner gave a short nod. 'None of this grand nonsense everyone does at weddings. We may be vampires, but that does not mean we need to be over-the-top.'

Olivia wanted to tell her that it sort of *did*. They were, after all, hosting the wedding of the century – in a *mansion*. This was not the time to be skimping with one measly pianist!

'Besides,' the woman went on, pursing her lips, 'for youngsters like Alex and Tessa, this will simply be their *first* wedding. They can go over-the-top with their second and third ones!'

Olivia gasped. Of all the people to be so

cynical, it was the wedding planner? By rights she ought to be one of the most romantic people on earth. *In fact*, thought Olivia, her face growing hot, *she should be making every effort to ensure that this is the most wonderful day ever for Alex and Tessa. She's acting more like a Wedding Witch than a Wedding Planner!*

And if the Wedding Witch got her way, Tessa and Alex would be getting married in a blandly decorated Great Hall with only one man on the piano to serenade them. Now, Olivia knew her taste was skewed a little pinker than the rest of the vampire world's, but no colour at all? She glanced at the crushed petals on the floor. At this rate, there were going to be no flowers at this wedding whatsoever. *That's about as wrong as wearing socks with sandals!* And wait, Tessa had even said she wanted the wedding day to be filled with flowers!

It was time for Olivia to do something. She

took a step out from her corner, planning to give her opinion as diplomatically as possible, when she felt a soft touch on her shoulder. She jumped. It was one of the servants, tall and ghostly pale, with a fabulous bright-red pixie haircut that Olivia knew she could never have pulled off. The vampire looked young – though it was hard for Olivia to tell an adult vampire's age – and she held a spool of black satin ribbon that she'd been looping along the hall's walls.

'Don't get involved,' the vampire said. 'Trust me.'

Olivia double-checked that the wedding planner was still ranting away so that she could whisper without fear of being overheard. 'But someone has to stop her or else she's going to ruin everything. Why is she even a wedding planner if she hates romance so much?'

The Pixie Vampire leaned closer. 'She's not usually like this.'

Olivia looked back at the wedding planner. The black clothes, the sombre decorations, the lone pianist – she seemed to be taking anything romantic and doing the exact opposite . . . as if she was making a statement . . .

'What's the wedding planner's name?' she asked Pixie Vampire, feeling an idea bubbling in her brain.

'Her name's Lucia. But I'm telling you, if you get in her way, she'll eat you for breakfast.' Pixie Vampire sniffed Olivia. 'With you, maybe literally.'

Olivia shuddered. It wasn't easy being the only human in a room full of vampires. Olivia took a breath and walked up the aisle. She gently linked her arm through Lucia's stony vampire arm, drawing her close. 'I love your idea for the lone pianist,' she said. 'It's just so classy. And who can argue with the timeless appeal of black?' Lucia gave a thin smile, bowing her head graciously. 'But do you think that you're in danger of making the day look slightly . . . mournful? Lone pianists always remind me of that film where the actress plays a heartbroken woman, sitting on her own in the ball room where she was due to get married.' She looked long and hard at Lucia. 'It must be awful for someone to feel like that.'

Lucia turned her head away and Olivia heard a muffled sob. 'Come here,' Olivia said, drawing the wedding planner to her in a hug. To her surprise, Lucia didn't pull away, but buried her head in Olivia's shoulder.

'I just wasn't expecting it!' she said in a muffled voice.

'I know, I know,' Olivia said, comforting her.

'How did you guess?' Lucia asked, pulling back to look into Olivia's face.

'I could tell by the way you were fidgeting and touching the ring finger of your left hand. There was a ring on there until very recently, wasn't there?'

A sniffle escaped the sophisticated vampire and, when she turned to face Olivia, tears were pooling in her eyes. Suddenly, Olivia was *very* aware that a hush had fallen over the Great Hall. Every servant had stopped working and was now watching the scene unfold.

Lucia sank down into one of the plush chairs arranged for the guests. She wiped her eyes, smudging her eyeliner. 'I don't know what's got into me,' she whimpered. 'I feel so stupid for crying over such a heartless . . . *cad*.'

Olivia sat down beside her, taking Lucia's hand in her lap. 'Can you tell me what happened?'

Lucia blinked back more tears. 'I was engaged.' Her chin dropped to her chest. 'I was supposed to have a beautiful wedding, just like the one tomorrow.' Lucia's breathing was shaky. 'But at the last moment he called it off. It was only a month ago. My whole life fell apart.' Her lower lip quivered and Olivia worried she was about to start real, full-on sobbing. Olivia patted her hand, noticing that even Lucia's fingernails were painted black.

'I'm sorry to hear that. That truly is the worst! A cancelled wedding! I can't even imagine. When you must have been dreaming of your wedding day – with the veil and the big white dress and beautiful bouquets!' Olivia noticed Lucia glaring at her. 'Sorry,' she said, returning to her train of thought. 'But surely no, erm, *cad* is worth abandoning your entire faith in romance for, right?'

Lucia sniffled, but didn't disagree.

'Listen,' continued Olivia. 'I remember when I was in Hollywood and another actress tried to ruin my big moment. But was I going to let someone else get the better of me?' Olivia paused for a response.

'No?' Lucia finally hiccupped.

'Of course not!' Olivia said with a touch more

oomph. 'And what about you? Should you let some guy get the upper hand?'

'I guess not,' Lucia squeaked.

'*Absolutely* not,' said Olivia, feeling like she was in the middle of a very important pep rally. She pulled Lucia back on to her feet. 'The best way to get over your loser ex would be to celebrate the very idea of romance with a wedding fit for a prince and princess. How often do you get to throw a royal wedding? And think of the thrill it will give Tessa and Alex when they see all you've done.'

'You're right.' Lucia swallowed hard, gesturing to the greenhouse lady, who was cradling her half-empty basket by the wall. 'Helga, let me see those flower samples one more time.'

Olivia watched Lucia sniff a bright purple bloom. *All in a day's work*, she thought, mentally patting herself on the back. As the Great Hall began to bustle again, this time with more energetic activity, she slipped outside through the giant French doors.

My own love life may be on 'pause' for the time being, but that doesn't mean I can't help fix other people's. As she wound her way through the long corridors of the Lazar mansion, Olivia realised that she should have felt positively giddy at her triumph. She had helped *save the day*!

But instead of being happy and light, she still felt like a heavy weight had settled in the depths of her stomach. The sound of her wedge sandals ricocheted along the empty hallways, giving Olivia a hollow feeling. She missed Jackson, with his megawatt smile and sweet blue eyes that made her feel like she was melting. But that wasn't all. As Olivia wandered aimlessly among the ancestral portraits and ornate wallpaper, she realised that maybe one day Ivy might have her own wedding in this very building. *Maybe she'll never return to Franklin Grove.* Olivia felt so isolated it was as if she was living on the outskirts of Siberia. Even when she tried to take her mind off Jackson or Ivy, there was no escaping the fear that was quickly becoming all too real to Olivia. She'd only recently got to know this whole new side to her family, and now it felt as though it was all being snatched away again.

I might be left on my own, she thought. *I might lose my sister.*

Chapter Six

Ivy stuffed another tender piece of rare steak into her mouth. She and Petra were seated at a round, granite table inside the Wallachia canteen. Unlike at Franklin Grove, where the students ate off plastic trays with flimsy forks, Wallachia provided fancy cloth napkins and baroque silverware. The table setting was even nicer than her father's best china at home!

'You like it?' asked Petra, shoving some food around on her plate.

'Like it? The food here is ten times better than anything at the Meat and Greet and the Bloodmart back home, *combined* – and, trust me,' she said with her mouth full, 'I'm a big fan of both.'

'American food . . .' Petra sighed as if a plate of burgers and French fries might be the most exotic thing on the planet. 'You're so lucky!'

Lucky? Ivy was about to disagree entirely when she took a sip of straight B-positive from the crystal goblet in front of her, grimacing the way humans did when they sucked a lemon. 'OK, fine, I'll admit, you guys may be lacking in the milkshake department.' Ivy preferred to get her blood fix a little less directly.

'Well,' said Petra, 'if you came here permanently, I'm sure the chef could figure out something as simple as a milkshake. But seriously –' she pointed her fork at Ivy – 'we need more cool, less stuck-up girls around, and having you here would be a *big* help.'

Ivy felt her face get hot. 'Thanks,' she stammered. Ivy thought Petra was cool, too, but how stuck-up *was* this place if Petra was so desperate to balance out the snoot-factor?

Just then a group of first years walked by in their Wallachia uniforms – each with a matching strand of pearls. Their red pleated skirts swung lightly at their knees. As if on cue, their heads swivelled to examine Ivy. *Oh no, do I have something in my teeth?* Ivy slid her tongue over her would-be fangs, but that wasn't it. A blonde first year with a trendy designer tote bag wrinkled her nose, her gaze lingering on Ivy's plain T-shirt and jeans. She was worse than Charlotte Brown – even worse than the old, prima-donna version of Charlotte before she had become kind of, sort of, Ivy's friend.

The moment the girls were out of earshot, Petra burst into laughter. 'Oh my darkness, you *so* have to come here!'

'After that?' asked Ivy. 'Where I come from, that wouldn't exactly pass for a warm welcome.'

Petra clutched her sides. 'Can you *imagine* how

riled up those girls will be every single day if you come here? It's going to be killer.' She squeezed Ivy's arm as if the two of them had concocted this whole scheme together.

'Right,' said Ivy, pulling her hands to her lap. 'Killer . . .' But her neck prickled. Could it be that Petra wasn't as friendly as she'd thought? It seemed like she just hoped that Ivy's American ways would get a rise out of the teachers and the other snooty students.

Ivy was about to excuse herself when the sound of a loud gong rippled through the air. She looked around. Why would someone be ringing a gong? Everyone but Ivy jumped up. An excited murmur travelled through the canteen, the likes of which Ivy hadn't seen since Principal Whitehead had announced the school dance at the end of term and the bunnies had freaked out. Could that be it? Was there going to be a Wallachia-style shindig?

'Hey! That sound can mean only one thing – a duel! Come on.' Petra pulled Ivy up by the sleeve of her T-shirt. 'We don't want to miss this. It's pretty much the only time boys and girls are allowed to mix!'

A duel? Ivy wondered. *Like, to the death?* Petra dragged her outside to a grassy field where a group of vampire boys were bunched together. A bunch of girls were huddled together too, whispering furiously to each other, their eyes wide. *Haven't they ever seen boys before?* Ivy thought. *If this is the way that segregated classes make girls behave I'm not sure I like it.*

One of the boys suddenly slammed a rugby ball to the ground, where it bounced – or it would have bounced, had it not burst.

'What's going on?' asked Ivy, going on tiptoes because the crowd outside was getting so thick. Two young vampire boys snatched off their shirts while their fellow players formed a tight ring around them. Ivy caught her breath. The Academy might be fancy, but it wasn't all that different from Franklin Grove School. *Stupid teen boys on an ego trip – it must be universal.*

The onlookers had drawn closer, chanting: 'Fight! Fight! Fight!'

All across the grounds more students were streaming on to the field. 'We need a better view.' Petra tugged Ivy along after her again, snaking through the crowd until they found a perch on a stone bench. 'You're in luck!' Petra winked. 'We don't get one of these every day, you know!' Petra clapped her hands and began whooping along with the other spectators. 'I love duels,' she continued. 'There aren't enough of them these days. Seriously, we've gone whole school years without one.'

In the centre of the ring of vampires, the two boys, shirtless and barefoot, circled each other. They looked high-school age, around sixteen. One of them – the slightly taller one – was tying his long blond hair into a ponytail, while the other removed an expensive-looking gold watch and handed it to one of his friends standing nearby.

Ivy was finding the whole scene strange. The boys back at Franklin Grove would shout and get furious and shove each other – but these boys were calm and focused. They didn't even look that angry. Ivy shuddered. This wouldn't be a regular human fight. Knowing vampire skills the way Ivy did, she knew this could turn out very, very badly. Ivy tried not to imagine the damage the two boys could do to one another.

Another commotion stirred the crowd and the ring parted opposite her and Petra. Now everyone was gasping. Prince Alex stepped right into the circle with the shirtless vampires. Everyone bowed in his presence, including the two fighters. Ivy's shoulders relaxed. Everything would be under control now. Alex would put a stop to this.

The prince wedged himself between the two boys, one palm on each of their chests. 'It's fortunate that I'm here today. Please state your names.' Alex's voice boomed across the field.

'Carlos,' answered the tall, blond vampire.

'Gregor,' said the shorter one.

'And what is your quarrel?'

Gregor pointed at his opponent, a sneer twisting his lips. 'Carlos accused me of dishonesty on the playing field, but he's wrong. *I* took the lead fairly –' he pushed his finger into his chest – 'and *I* should not be called a cheat in front of my classmates.'

Carlos shook his head and his ponytail swept across his bare back. 'That's not what happened. I saw the ball touch the ground but Gregor carried on playing – he had an unfair advantage.'

'You're mistaken,' Gregor insisted.

'I am not.' Carlos crossed his arms. Ivy rolled her eyes. They were being so polite, while still managing to act like total *cavemen*. Were they really going to fight over *this*? Ivy would give them each a trophy if they would just chill out!

Alex turned to the group. 'Would the other players please step forward?' Young vampires wearing different coloured Wallachia rugby shirts entered the circle, bowing slightly as they approached Prince Alex. 'Now. Can anyone verify either boy's story?'

They all shrugged. One bulky vampire with huge, muddied hands spoke up for the group. 'It all happened too fast and we were playing the game ourselves. We didn't get a good look.'

'Very well,' said Prince Alex, returning to the two quarrelling players. 'As the highest-ranking vampire on this property, I hereby formally sanction this duel.'

What!? Ivy nearly blurted out. *He can't be serious.* Alex was supporting the boys' decision to fight? It didn't make sense! Ivy started to push forwards

– there would be no duel if she had anything to say about it – but Petra grabbed her arm and pulled it back down to her side, giving Ivy a look that said, *Don't even think about it.*

But why? Ivy wanted to know. She didn't want to watch a vampire fight and she couldn't understand why anyone else would want to either. These boys could seriously hurt each other. And since when did Ivy Vega bite her tongue about anything?

'Is this a joke?' Ivy demanded in Petra's ear. 'We can't actually be about to watch two boys fight each other, can we?'

'Shhh!' Petra pressed a finger to her lips. 'It's tradition! And I'd take this over an action movie any day. I only wish I'd known. I'd have grabbed us a box of plasmallows!'

Ivy's stomach did a nosedive. *If I didn't know for a fact that I have excellent hearing, I'd think I needed my ears checked.*

A younger vampire boy drew a circle with a stick around the shirtless boys, who were crouched opposite one another. Ivy squirmed beside Petra. Were they really going to go through with this 'duel'?

Like a radio announcer, Alex began to outline the rules. 'Each opponent must respect the rules of the duel,' he began. 'One: there will be three rounds. Two: in each round one vampire must try to push the other vampire out of the circle. Three: no punching or biting is allowed in the fight. Four: as referee, my word is law. My say is final. And five: if at the end of the third and final round there is no clear victor, we will return tomorrow at the same time for a rematch . . . with swords. Agreed?'

The crowd exploded into rowdy cheering as if their favourite team had just scored a goal. Vampire boys pumped their fists in the air while the girls who had stared at Ivy began a high-pitched chant: 'Greg-or, Greg-or, Greg-or!' The ringleader of the group lifted her palms in the air, trying to encourage more people to join in.

Gregor and Carlos bent low, fingers grazing the ground and muscles tense. Petra's hand tightened around Ivy's arm. *We are* not *in this together*, thought Ivy and she shrugged off Petra's grip, pushing her way out of the crowd. She didn't know where she was heading to; she just knew she didn't want to stay here.

She stumbled out of the mass of vampires, winding up near the front gates of the school where her grandmother had dropped her off not too long ago. She had thought vampires were more advanced than bunnies. They were stronger and quicker and had super-senses, but that didn't change the fact that they were so old-fashioned they were practically backwards! Of all the ways vampires could use their physical superiority, they chose to waste it on dumb things like this –

a *duel*! Ivy felt sick, like she'd swallowed a whole clove of garlic.

She climbed on to a cool stone bench, pulling her knees to her chest. The students were still whooping, though at least from here Ivy could no longer see Carlos and Gregor. *It's like the Middle Ages never ended for these people.*

Ivy stared through the wrought-iron gate with its regal Wallachia crest. If this was the way young vampires were expected to behave at the Academy, Ivy wasn't sure she could ever be proud to wear it.

Ivy's head snapped up at the sound of a door opening behind her. Three teachers in long professorial robes sprinted out in the direction of the fight. The first of them – a thin, pointy-nosed teacher – noticed Ivy sitting on the bench. She skidded to a stop. 'Come on!' she said. 'The duel might be over at any moment. You certainly don't want to be the only one to miss it, now do you?'

Actually I do, she wanted to tell them. Ivy couldn't believe it. Had she entered a parallel universe? She pinched herself to be sure she wasn't dreaming. But when she blinked and saw that she was still seated in the middle of the pristine grounds, Ivy decided to smile and wave the teachers on. After all, challenging centuries of convention was a bit too much to take on during a simple school visit.

Even for Ivy Vega.

Chapter Seven

Olivia may not have had any vamp powers, but she had competed in the state cheerleading competition three times, and that meant she had a few special skills of her own. She stared up at the impossibly high oak tree. Its branches stretched over the Lazar family grounds. It was the perfect spot to scout for locations for shots of the wedding reception . . . just so long as she didn't look down.

Olivia straddled the tree trunk and inched her way up until she reached one of the solid lower branches. From there, she caught hold of the next limb up, moving from bough to bough like she was climbing a rickety ladder. When she reached a branch near the top of the tree, she hiked her leg over and leaned her back against the knotted trunk.

Her feet dangled as she lifted the viewfinder to study the landscape. The first half of the wedding reception was to be held outside, beneath the sparkling Transylvania stars, before the guests went back into the ballroom to dance the night away. The whole day was going to be a fairytale come true – only this fairytale came with vampires. The tables had been draped with garlands of pink-and-cream flowers. A silk awning billowed over the table where Tessa and Alex would sit for the wedding dinner, and a band was setting up to one side, their gilt chairs decorated with huge cream satin bows. *I'm so glad Lucia changed her plans*, she thought. *All it took was a nudge in the right direction.*

Olivia snapped a few test shots, double-checking the digital screen after each one to see which angles were working best. She scooted further out along the branch, but then it dawned on her: *I'll hardly be able to climb up here in the fabulous gown I'll be wearing!* Not that she'd ever tested it, but Olivia didn't think pink chiffon and rough tree bark would go together very well.

The branch swayed beneath her and she dug all ten fingernails into the tree until the bough stopped moving. Panting, Olivia smacked herself on the forehead. What was wrong with her lately? Was she so desperate to avoid thinking about Jackson that she would risk life and limb climbing a stupid tree? She needed to get it together. She clutched the trunk and lowered herself on to a branch below.

Crack!

Olivia felt rotting bark crumble beneath her feet, and she slipped down. She managed to grasp a sturdier branch above her, clutching it with her fingertips. Her feet swished wildly through thin air. She looked up at the branch she was holding for dear life.

Don't panic, Olivia. Do not panic. She squeezed her eyes shut. Too late – she was totally panicking. Her arms started to shake and her fingers were aching with the strain of holding on. *I could really use a dose of that super-strength about now!* Where was her sister when she needed her? Olivia tried to adjust her grip, but her hand slipped and her stomach virtually jumped into her mouth. Down she plummeted.

'Heeeeeeeelp! *Ooof!*'

She landed in a clumsy heap on the ground, cradling her camera to her chest. *How utterly great*, she thought. *I try to stay busy and I wind up nearly killing myself!* Olivia stretched her arms and then her legs, flexing her wrists and ankles. She'd had enough practice tumbling from the top of a cheer pyramid to manage not to break any bones.

At least she could be thankful for that, and the camera was still in one piece.

Something in the grass prickled her shins, and Olivia scooted back. She looked down at the spot where she had landed. She was up to her ankles in exotic plants with green, ivy-like vines and furry white blossoms. Almost instantly, her skin started to itch. She leaned down to scratch, but the itching was getting worse by the second. She straightened up to get out of reach of the devilish plants, but then she noticed that she was bang in the middle of a crop; there was another metre's worth of plants between her and the clear grass.

It was time for Olivia's cheerleader skills again. She took two steps back, squared her shoulders and catapulted herself into the air, performing a perfect somersault before landing free and clear of the plant beds.

As she dusted off her clothes, Helga the Greenhouse Lady appeared at her side. 'My dear, are you all right? I saw you fall into the . . . into the . . . Oh, no!' She was staring at the crushed bed of plants at the base of the tree.

'I'm sorry. I didn't mean to damage them. It was an accid–'

But before Olivia could finish, Helga grabbed her round the waist and slung her over her shoulder! 'I don't care what you've done to the plants, it's what the plants have done to you!' she gasped.

'Wha– what's going on?' Olivia cried as the woman broke into a run. Her body jiggled painfully against the gardener's collar bone. Helga was racing back to the greenhouse with her as cargo! All she could do was watch the scenery go by as if in fast-forward. Helga pushed through a glass door, which grazed Olivia's hair as it slammed shut behind them.

'Don't worry, don't worry,' Helga muttered under her breath, setting Olivia down on a metal table covered with various garden tools and bags of loose soil. 'I have just the thing for you.'

For me?

Olivia stared open-mouthed at the high-tech greenhouse surrounding her. Artificial rain poured down from shiny, silver trays over rows of lush plants, complete with a soundtrack of rolling thunder. A miniature blimp buzzed around a track, sprinkling coloured fertiliser, and Olivia listened as giant, metal turbines mixed mulch in the corner.

Meanwhile, Helga bustled around, opening cabinets and grabbing colourful bottles. Olivia wanted to tell her that she wasn't actually worried at all, but the woman seemed so concerned that Olivia thought it might be best to leave her alone.

'I've only just started working here.' Helga sniffed a purple bottle. 'So I don't quite know where everything is kept yet.' She opened another steel cabinet and peered inside. 'Ah, here it is!'

Helga wetted a strip of gauze with yellow liquid from a silver jar and began scrubbing Olivia's legs with it.

'Oh my goodness!' Olivia looked down at her legs. Now she saw why Helga was worried. Her legs had changed colour from tanned to an angry red. A mass of swollen lumps had risen up on her shins. 'What happened to me?' she asked. While Helga scrubbed, Olivia scratched, but nothing could stop the terrible itching that was crawling up the length of her legs. *Ew, a rash!* She hoped it wasn't contagious.

'You got yourself caught in a crop of Bloodbite Nettles,' Helga told her. Olivia groaned – even the name of the plant sounded painful! Helga wetted the gauze again and continued rubbing.

Olivia wanted to tell Helga that she was sorry about crushing the nettles, but all that came out was a long wheezing breath. She reached for her throat. Her lungs felt raw and swollen. She couldn't speak. She waved her hands wildly at Helga.

'Oh dear.' Helga cleared the table of gardening tools. 'Lie down.' Olivia obeyed. 'Yes, put your legs up, that's right. Unfortunately, Bloodbite Nettles can have this effect.'

I wish those things had come with a warning label, thought Olivia, her chest heaving.

Helga rested an icy vampire hand on Olivia's forehead. 'Just lie very still and this will pass.' Olivia blinked twice in response.

The greenhouse door was flung open and in burst Horatio. 'I was washing the car and saw you rush in with Olivia. Miss Olivia, are you OK?'

Olivia rolled her head to the side and tried to smile, but she couldn't because her face was swelling like she'd been stung by a whole swarm of bees. She knew Horatio must have been lingering nearby in the hopes of seeing Helga.

After all, he had arrived very quickly – even for a vampire.

'She'll be fine,' said Helga. She glanced sideways at Horatio, who was standing there like he didn't know what to do with his hands – just like he had done during the car ride to the airport. 'Would you mind passing me that corked bottle to your left?' Helga asked. Their fingers brushed as Horatio passed the bottle and Olivia thought she noticed the faintest hint of a quiver run through the butler. 'Thank you.'

Helga was grinding herbs into a thick paste that let out noisy squelches each time she stirred. She pointed and Horatio passed and, with each new solution added to the gooey mix, the smell wafting out of the bowl became more and more foul.

'Once you drink this –' Helga held up a spoonful of slimy, dripping goop – 'you'll feel one thousand times better.'

Drink? Olivia tried to let out a groan but her

throat was now so swollen that making any kind of noise was out of the question. Horatio took a step forwards, opening his mouth to say something, but then stopped and retreated again. Helga turned just in time to see Horatio step back.

'Oh, were you about to –'

'No, I just . . .' Horatio wrung his hands.

'Oh, right, well I'd better . . .' Helga trailed off and went back to stirring. Horatio, normally a giant, seemed suddenly shorter. Olivia frowned with frustration. *If only I could talk! I would get those two chatting away in no time!* But her tongue was filling her entire mouth and anything she managed to garble would have come out as nonsense. Not to mention the fact that the allergic reaction was boggling her brain, too! What if she couldn't breathe? What if she swelled up into a big balloon and floated away? All while Horatio and Helga were making googly-eyes at one another.

OK, calm down, Olivia. Focus on the positive. She

tried to relax and redirect her thoughts towards something more productive.

For instance, Olivia *had* managed to get these two together and talking – in a way. So what if she had only been trying to take her mind off Jackson? It didn't matter, because Helga and Horatio would make the cutest vampire couple ever!

H + H . . . How sweet!

Helga turned to pour her mixture into a glass as Horatio helped Olivia sit up. She jerked her head in Helga's direction, lifting her eyebrows as if to tell him, *Go on*, say *something!* Why couldn't she be telepathic?

Horatio squinted, staring at Olivia. Olivia jerked her head again, but Horatio just peered closer.

'Come quickly,' he said, 'I think something is wrong with Miss Olivia!' Olivia tried to shake her head. *You're missing the point!*

Helga came over to look at Olivia, bringing the glass of smelly herb sludge with her. At least

Olivia's plan had sort of worked. Helga and Horatio were now standing next to each other – that was *something*.

'She'll be fine once she drinks this,' Helga said, handing Olivia the glass.

Bottoms up! Olivia pinched her nose and took a swig. It had to be one of the most disgusting things she had ever tasted. She would rather swallow a tubful of Charlotte Brown's fake tan than drink this stuff. But immediately the swelling in her tongue started to go down, and the hot itching in her legs began to fade. *Phew!*

Helga grabbed a sack from the other side of the greenhouse and propped it under Olivia's head so that she could lie back down – which was good, because she felt like she was going to need a moment to digest the horrible medicine.

Olivia rested in the humid air of the greenhouse, breathing in the scent of fresh soil and flowers. Horatio and Helga stood on either side of the table, gazing at each other. Suddenly, Olivia was a little grossed out. She wanted Horatio to be happy, but what if those two leaned over her to have their first kiss?

Um – ew!

As Olivia's eyelids started to grow heavy from the medicine, Helga turned away from Horatio with nothing more than a shy smile. Olivia drifted off to sleep, unable to keep her eyes open any more.

Getting Horatio and Helga together would have to wait.

Ivy's combat boots had rubbed penny-sized blisters on her feet and she was seriously thinking about asking to borrow Olivia's ballet flats for the rest of the weekend. She had taken a bus back from Wallachia Academy and was now making the long trek up the country road leading to the Lazar family's massive front gate.

The sun was a burning orb hanging low in the Transylvania sky, and a light breeze tousled the bullrushes growing alongside the road. Ivy knew she should feel lucky. She was taking a walk in one of the most scenic countries in the world before getting to attend a real, live royal wedding. But it was hard to enjoy herself when she knew she might have to stay here indefinitely. Instead of making her feel better about staying in Transylvania, her tour of Wallachia had been a total disaster!

Ivy kicked a pebble and watched it skitter along. Then she looked up to see a vamp so obvious, he might as well have been wearing a cape . . . Wait – he *was* wearing a cape! How utterly lame! She wouldn't have thought that Transylvania, home of the vampires, would have its very own version of the Beasts. It was like looking into a crystal ball and seeing Garrick Stephens' future. The vampire was walking towards her down the rural road, stopping every once in a while to stare past the fence and into the Lazars' estate. *What in Dracula's name is he doing?*

Ivy flashed a brief smile as she passed the over-the-top vampire. He flung his cape over his shoulder with a big *whoosh* and lowered his chin in acknowledgment. 'My Lady,' he said.

'Um, hi!' Ivy ground her teeth together, stifling her laughter. The vamp's long, dark hair was arranged in what she could only describe as a well-maintained mullet. If only Olivia were here to see – this man was a walking crime against fashion! *Yuck.*

She walked on, almost grateful to the OTT vampire. He had made her laugh despite her funk. Once she'd got beyond the creaky gates, Ivy walked through the grounds, looking at the trimmed hedges shaped like bats and the stone fountains gushing impossibly blue water into lily ponds. A man in a black suit and with a Bluetooth connected to his ear stopped her at the front door.

'Ma'am, may I ask who you are?' He held up white-gloved hands to stop her from entering.

'Seriously?' she asked. 'I'm Ivy . . .' He stared at her blankly. 'Ivy Vega . . . You know, the Countess's granddaughter . . . from America.'

'One moment while I verify, please.' The man murmured into the Bluetooth, 'Ivy Vega is here, Countess Lazar. May she enter?' Then to Ivy: 'Very sorry, Miss Vega. Please, come right in. Welcome back.'

'Thanks.' Ivy smoothed her face into a serious expression. 'I'll try my best to behave.'

She hurried into the house, wanting to catch up with Olivia right away, and find out why their grandparents' house had suddenly become Fort Knox. She was in need of some serious sisterly venting time. Stuck-up vamps, a pathetic duel and a long walk home – there was a lot to get through. As she looked for Olivia, Ivy passed the Countess's study. The door was half open so she peeked inside.

'No, no, no!'

The Queen was pacing the room, her posture as straight as a chopstick. *So that's why the mansion has turned into an army camp*, she realised. *The Queen is an ultra-stressed Mother of the Groom!*

'Everything is wrong.' She adjusted her jewelled crown. 'The forest-green aisle runner clashes completely with the emerald necklace you will be wearing. Surely you don't want to walk down the aisle to the "Bridal Chorus" surrounded by colour clashes! No, we absolutely cannot have that. It must be perfect. This is my only son's wedding we're talking about.'

As Ivy hovered at the door, she saw Tessa sitting in a chair, taking notes in the corner. Tessa's eyes had shadows under them and her hair fell lankly around her face. *She looks worn out.*

'Maybe it's better to keep things simple then,' suggested Tessa in a meek voice that sounded nothing like that of a soon-to-be princess. 'Alex and I could get married in a quiet ceremony somewhere else and return here for the reception.'

The hope in Tessa's suggestion floated like a bubble in the air and, sure enough, the Queen popped it with one dismissive flourish of her ringed hand. 'That is not *tradition*.'

Ivy rolled her eyes. She was beginning to wonder about all these vampire customs. They seemed so rigid. Maybe she would be better off in Franklin Grove, where the most serious tradition was singing embarrassing Christmas carols at the school's Winter Assembly. As far as she could tell, the Transylvania vamps needed to take a chill pill!

Before the Queen or Tessa noticed her, Ivy snuck up to the second floor and slipped into the bedchamber she shared with Olivia. The room was empty, but right now Ivy was too tired to worry about it. The events of the day had suddenly caught up with her and all she wanted was a nice, long nap – preferably before *she* got roped into any party-planning.

She opened her coffin lid and was about to climb in when she noticed it was already occupied!

'Olivia?' She shook her sister. Olivia was lying in the coffin with her arms folded across her chest. 'What are you *doing*?'

Olivia sat up, shielding her eyes from the light. 'Huh?' She squinted at Ivy almost as if she didn't recognise her.

'What are you doing in my coffin?' Ivy cocked her head, a little worried now. Her twin looked pasty and pale – but, then again, Transylvania wasn't quite as sunny as Franklin Grove.

'I'm sorry.' Olivia spoke as if it was an effort. 'I didn't have the energy to climb into my own bunk. I figured you wouldn't mind if I took a nap in yours.'

Ivy smiled. 'Of course not. It just gave me a scare seeing you in my coffin like that. You were sleeping like the dead!'

'It's surprisingly comfortable,' said Olivia, nestling back into the red velour cushioning. She closed her eyes. 'Would you mind shutting the lid?'

Wow, the jet lag must have really caught up with her, thought Ivy as she gently closed the lid on her human twin. Bunnies were more vulnerable to that sort of thing, Ivy knew. There was probably no need to worry. Olivia just needed a good nap and maybe a cup of coffee to jump-start her into Transylvania time.

The bedroom door was flung open, making Ivy jump. 'Shhh! Olivia's going to sleep!' Then she saw it was Tessa.

'Sorry!' Tessa whispered. 'Can I hide out here for a bit?'

'Yeah, no problem.' Ivy offered her the swivel chair at the desk. Tessa's hair was in tangles and her mascara was smudged under her eyes. Suddenly, Ivy wished Olivia could be more . . . well, *awake*. Her sister watched every one of those wedding shows. She would be much better at comforting a clearly stressed-out bride.

Ivy sat on the floor, playing with her shoelaces. What if she said the wrong thing? 'Um, is everything OK, Tessa? You seem, sort of, all over the place?' She cringed. That hadn't come out right.

'Huh? Me?' Tessa's eyes flicked up. She'd been staring into space. 'I'm fine. Just typical wedding craziness.'

'I guess that's to be expected when you're planning the wedding of the century.' Ivy tried to smile before she became tongue-tied again. The two sat in uncomfortable silence.

Ivy glanced up and saw Olivia's camera on the

desk by the computer. Olivia had been diligently snapping pictures ever since they'd arrived. It reminded Ivy that she should be doing more for her article. It wasn't going to write itself! But now hardly seemed like the right time to interview Tessa.

Then Ivy had another idea. She stood up and picked the camera off the desk. 'Do you want to check out Olivia's pictures? Maybe it will take your mind off all the crazy wedding stuff for a bit.'

Tessa gave a tired smile. 'OK.'

'Great.' Ivy pushed the power button and the screen lit up. 'If I know my sister, she'll have taken some killer shots.'

Sitting together on the narrow swivel chair, Ivy scrolled through the photos. There was a stunning picture of the rose meadow, and one of the mansion reflected in the glinting glass of the greenhouse. Olivia really did have an eye for this sort of thing. She had used different camera features to brighten the colours and the natural lighting to highlight certain parts of the scenery. If anything, Olivia had made the house and grounds look even more spectacular than they appeared in real life.

But what – or, *who* – was that in the background? Tessa craned her neck to take a closer look. Ivy leaned in, absorbed in Olivia's shot. There was a figure lurking on the edge of the screen. She clicked the zoom button twice. It was the OTT caped vampire that she had run into on the side of the road. In the shot Olivia had taken, he was standing in a clump of tall bushes. *Somebody's taking this creepy horror-movie shtick too far*, thought Ivy, noticing that in the picture he was staring up towards the castle. What was he doing?

'That is the weirdest thing. I ran into that same guy on the road outside the palace,' Ivy explained, staring at the shadowy figure lurking in the background of Olivia's photo. 'Total creepazoid, if you know what I mean. Do you think we should tell someone? I'm sure you don't want anyone gate-crashing your big day.'

But when Ivy turned, Tessa was gone. Vanished. What was that about? Did Tessa know the guy in the picture? No – no way *that* guy could know a soon-to-be-princess. Maybe Tessa had just remembered some last-minute detail she had to attend to before the big day. Ivy didn't know the first thing about weddings, so that was entirely possible. But why would she run off without saying a word?

This royal wedding was really beginning to mess with people's heads!

Chapter Eight

So much food and so little desire to eat it! Olivia knew this rehearsal dinner for the wedding was going to be totally wasted on her. She rested her elbow on the arm of her chair and pushed her cheek into her palm. Buttery rolls, smoked-salmon roulades and miniature quiches were piled high on silver platters, but tonight, nothing could tempt her.

She should have been enjoying the candlelit banquet, but instead she was weak and clammy. Everything felt so distant – even Ivy and her bio-dad seemed a mile off, and they were on *either side* of her!

Lillian's voice came from the other side of Charles. 'The candelabra are just lovely. And *who* put together those gorgeous star-gazer arrangements?' She sounded tinny and far away. It was like Olivia was living in a dream within a dream.

Jet lag plus Helga's potion – which had to be the most vile thing she'd ever put in her mouth, including a non-vegetarian sausage she'd picked up by mistake at Ivy's house that summer – were proving to be a powerful combination. She would be OK soon – any moment now. She just needed to catch her second wind, that was all. Perhaps she could distract herself by sharing her secret theory with Ivy.

'Guess what?' she whispered, leaning over to her twin. 'I think there's another romance blossoming here. I'm sure Horatio has a crush on the gardener, Helga.' Before she could go into more detail she noticed something across the room. 'Hey. What's with Tessa?' she asked. The bride-to-be was staring glassy-eyed into the distance, not paying a bit of attention to any of the conversations going on around her. She seemed in even more of a funk than Olivia.

'I don't know,' said Ivy, whose chunky black bracelets jangled as she took another helping of chocolate marshmallow platelets for dessert. 'It's weird. She came to our room to hide out while you were napping. One moment she was there and the next she had run out of the bedchamber without saying a word. This wedding must be really getting to her.'

'Seriously? She ran out?' Olivia remembered how Tessa had run out on her own party last night too, like she hadn't wanted to be there. Olivia had thought it was wedding nerves, but now she knew that there was definitely something going on. *The question is: what can it be?*

Prince Alex reached for Tessa's hand, but

she pulled it away to fiddle with her hair and then placed it firmly in her lap. Oh no! Had they argued? That would make the most sense, but they were usually such a happy pair. Was the wedding going to be called off? Olivia stopped herself, realising that she was letting her imagination run wild. But after everything that had happened with Jackson – not to mention her recent tumble – she didn't feel able to judge anything any more.

Prince Alex stood up, clinking his crystal goblet with a knife. His teeth were sparkling white as he smiled out at the dinner guests as if nothing was wrong. He wore a cream-coloured suit and a slender crimson tie. If he had lived in the States, he might have had an impressive career as a male model.

'Welcome, everyone.' He held his glass high and the room fell silent. 'I'm going to use my bad jokes tonight, since this is a *rehearsal* dinner and

I would much prefer to save my best material for the wedding toast tomorrow. I hope you can forgive me.' The group chuckled. 'As many of you know, my relationship with Tessa hasn't always been bats and blackness.'

'What does that mean?' Olivia whispered in Ivy's ear, confused.

Ivy hissed back: 'It means their relationship hasn't always been easy-peasy.'

'We kept our love secret for a long time,' Prince Alex continued, 'and it is only recently that we came out of the coffin.' Alex paused for a smattering of applause and laughter. 'But all jokes aside –' he turned to his bride-to-be – 'Tessa is like the Free Rose of Summer – rare and beautiful. And now that I've found her, I know my future.'

Olivia knew that if she were Tessa she'd be swooning at Alex's touching words. Drawn-out *awwws* sounded around the dining table. In fact, the only person not showing any real emotion was Tessa. Instead, the soon-to-be-princess was staring hard at her lap. Ivy and Olivia shared a look, but either Prince Alex didn't notice his fiancée's expression or he was very good at hiding his feelings.

'To Tessa!' He raised the glass to his lips and took a sip.

'To Tessa!' The guests echoed.

A moment later, the door to the Banquet Hall banged open and every head in the room swivelled to look. There was a short scuffle with a white-coated servant, and then a caped vampire with a slicked-back mullet burst into the room. Olivia recognised the intruder immediately. It was the same creepy vamp Ivy had pointed out on Olivia's camera just before they had come down! What was he doing here at Alex and Tessa's dinner?

The Queen's bodyguard appeared behind the caped vampire, shaking his head. 'He was lurking outside, Count Lazar,' he announced. 'I tried to stop him, but he slipped through. I am terribly sorry.' The caped vampire straightened his collar, smiling as if crashing a royal dinner was the most normal thing on the planet, and turned to address the twins' father.

'Hello, Karl, my old friend,' he said. 'It's been a detestably long time.'

Olivia saw the look on her bio-dad's face and gasped. She had never seen him like this before; dark and scary. He looked like an evil vampire in a B-list horror movie. It actually gave her the chills when suddenly he snarled, 'You!' and leapt to his feet, his chair scooting back across the floor. The room fell silent.

Olivia dared a glance at Ivy, but her twin sister just shrugged. *This guy* knows *our father?* Olivia thought. *How?*

'The nerve of that man,' whispered a tuxedoed vampire with a thick goatee.

'To prance around looking like a cheap

haunted-house prop! It's ludicrous.' A woman wearing scarlet satin gloves tossed her napkin on the table in disgust.

Ludicrous was exactly the right word. The caped vampire wore thick eyeliner. His hair was greased back, styled into a sharp 'V' on his forehead. The lining of his cape was silky red and he wore pointy-toed boots that laced up to his knees. Olivia had never seen a more atrocious outfit anywhere, let alone smack bang in the middle of the Transylvanian elite!

Charles's body was stiff and his expression was ice cold. There was anger in his voice as he finally addressed the caped vampire. 'A long time? It has not been nearly long enough, Vincenzo.'

'Please, Karl, don't be so dramatic. It's ancient history.' Olivia had no idea what 'It' was. Vincenzo scanned the table. 'Is Susannah not here? She could always calm you down when your temper started flaring. You can be so –' he waved a hand through the air – 'impetuous!'

Charles moved so fast that, to Olivia's eye, he practically teleported. He lunged for Vincenzo, teeth flashing, but Count Lazar and Horatio quickly placed themselves between him and the caped vampire.

'This is not the way,' said the Count. His old eyes looked sad, contrasting sharply with his festive red smoking jacket.

From her place at the head of the table, the Queen called, 'Karl – *Charles* – listen to your father. There is a time and place for duelling, but this is not it.'

Charles did not return to his seat. His fists clenched and unclenched at his sides. A vein pulsed at his neck. 'You are *not* going to ruin another wedding,' he said through gritted teeth. Olivia shrank back into her seat. Her normally super-cool bio-dad looked like he was about to lose it.

Vincenzo puffed his chest out. 'But I never –'

'No,' bellowed Charles. 'Not this time. Do you understand me?'

Vincenzo's shoulders slumped, and his cape skirted the floor. 'But it's *my* niece getting married tomorrow,' he said. 'I promised her father that I'd always be there for her. I took this promise seriously, even after he and I fell out.'

Ivy and Olivia took a sharp breath at the same time. *His niece?* Everyone's eyes were drawn to Tessa and guests began whispering to one another. Poor Tessa stared at the table, pink-faced.

Nobody said a word as Vincenzo stepped closer to the table. He bowed low, flourishing his black cape around him. 'My dear Tessa,' he said. 'I just want to help you celebrate your big day.' He lifted his chin, waiting for Tessa's response.

The Queen glanced from Vincenzo to Tessa and then back to Vincenzo. Olivia thought the

Queen looked as if she had just noticed a strand of hair floating in her soup.

Tessa's eyes sparkled with tears. 'There isn't going to be a big day,' she said, her voice quaking. 'At least not as long as *you're* around. Now if you'll excuse me, I must go.' She pushed back from the table and everyone stood up as a mark of respect. Alex tried to reach for her, but she brushed him aside.

'I'm sorry, Alex,' she said. 'I just need to be alone.'

Olivia heard a loud rip and saw that Tessa's luxurious golden gown had got caught under the chair, tearing a large hole in the train. Tessa held the torn fabric limply in her hand and a single sob broke from her lips before she rushed for the door.

'Tessa, wait!' Prince Alex called after her. He seemed at a loss to know what to do – chase his bride or deal with the unwanted intruder.

Does this mean the wedding is off? Olivia wondered. *How awful!*

But then she discovered she had more pressing concerns – like why the floor of the Banquet Hall was rising up to meet her and why she was seeing doubles of Ivy! She toppled over just as blackness covered her vision.

One moment Olivia was standing next to her, and the next Ivy saw her begin to crumple to the floor. In an instant, Ivy shot her hands out and caught her sister's limp body just before she fell flat on her face.

'Olivia!' she cried. Ivy's heart thudded in her chest and it felt like she couldn't get a breath of air into her lungs. 'Olivia, Olivia! What's going on?' Ivy cradled her sister's sagging body. Olivia's eyes were wide and blank and her mouth hung open like a guppy fish. 'Can somebody please help me?' she asked, frantic.

Much to her surprise, instead of coming to her aid, Ivy saw Horatio sprint *out* of the room. Could he really be that squeamish when her sister needed help?

Her dad and Lillian rushed to her side. Lillian pressed the back of her hand to Olivia's forehead. 'She's burning up,' she said. 'Do you think she's come down with something? We should get her up to your bedchamber.' She hooked one of Olivia's arms over her shoulders and let Ivy support her on the other side.

Vincenzo's face hovered over Ivy. 'I can be of service,' he said.

But Charles shot him a death-stare that Ivy would have had to practise for years to master. 'I can take care of my daughter, thank you very much.' His voice was icy. 'Maybe you should worry about your niece . . . or, better yet, you can help by disappearing altogether. You ruined one wedding years ago – please don't spoil a second one now.'

Vincenzo's mouth worked to form words. 'But . . . It wasn't . . . It wasn't my fault. You cannot besmirch my name like this. I have my honour to think of!' He flung his cloak over one shoulder and began to march from the room, as though he had decided something. Then he stopped dead at the sight of Prince Alex, whose piercing eyes seemed to dare him to say another word.

Alex grabbed Vincenzo's elbow and pulled him further away from the crowd surrounding Olivia. 'I don't know who you are, but you are clearly not welcome in this home.'

'Don't worry, my liege.' The last word dripped with sarcasm. 'I am already going.'

'I've had enough of this,' Charles muttered, overhearing the confrontation. With one glance back, the twins' father scooped up Olivia and carried her out of the room, Ivy and Lillian close behind.

Ivy tried to keep her breathing under control. *Please let Olivia be OK . . .*

Ivy sat cross-legged on the floor beside Olivia, who was spread out like a corpse on the floor. Lillian had taken Charles back downstairs, to find a cool drink for Olivia. Ivy held her sister's cold, sweaty hand and kept repeating: *She's going to be fine, she's going to be fine, she's going to be fine*, like one of Mr Abbott's Zen mantras. Ivy realised that she and her twin had been using the word 'fine' a lot in the past few days – usually at times when they were very definitely *not* fine.

She tried to shake the thought from her head. Olivia was probably just run down from the flight – or suffering from some kind of allergy. *No biggie.* Ivy nearly choked as she mentally borrowed one of her sister's phrases.

Olivia would be fixed up in no time. This was Transylvania, home of the vampires, they were supposed to be advanced in medicine. *They'll have something special to help her . . .*

Right?

Horatio hurried in with an older woman, carrying a black medical kit that would have looked sinister to Ivy if she weren't relying on it to make her sister better. So *that* was why Horatio had rushed out of the room – to get help! By the way the two of them stood close together, Ivy guessed this must be Helga, the gardener Olivia had been telling her about – the one Horatio had a crush on.

Helga looked from Olivia to Ivy, shaking her head and clucking her tongue. 'Now I see what the problem is.' She kneeled down next to Olivia's frail body, wringing her hands. 'I had no idea that Miss Olivia was human!'

Are you kidding? Ivy thought. What vamp would be caught dead wearing pink from head to toe and shimmery eyeshadow? She didn't say any of this to Helga, though. Right now, she needed the herbologist to focus on fixing her twin.

'How could I not realise?' Helga's lips were pressed into a thin line. 'It's just that I saw her doing a spectacular somersault and it seemed so quick and agile, I thought that she *must* be a vampire.'

'What somersault?' Ivy asked. She hadn't heard a word about any impromptu acrobatics and, besides, they were a bit far removed from Olivia's cheerleading practice for that sort of thing.

'The one after she fell out of the tree. I think she was trying not to squish any of my plants.' Helga shook her head. 'But all I cared about was that she was all right.'

Falling out of a tree? Performing somersaults? Apparently Olivia's day had been more eventful than she'd let on. Ivy smiled weakly. 'That's my sister for you.'

'So when she got the allergic reaction to the

Bloodbite Nettles, I gave her medicine meant for vampires instead of humans. *That's* why she passed out.'

'Oh no!' Ivy felt a stab of worry. 'That sounds serious. Can you help her?' She knew that any remedy meant for a vampire was probably three times weaker than one intended for humans, because vampires had faster, stronger immune systems. Olivia would have felt OK for a while, but then her symptoms would have come back – much stronger.

'You *have* to help her!' Ivy wanted to reach out and shake Helga, but the gardener was already busy pulling instruments out of her big black bag. She lined up different shaped bottles and bags of herbs on the floor. A bitter smell wafted up from the mix of Helga's ingredients. 'Oh yes.' Helga furrowed her brow and pressed her hand to Olivia's forehead. 'It can be fixed. I'm going to need some help doing it, that's all. And Horatio has already helped carry in my bag for me.' Her eyes flicked up to Horatio, who seemed to glow at the mention of his name.

'Count me in,' said Ivy, giving her sister's hand a squeeze. But Olivia was still out cold. Her fingers lay limp and lifeless in Ivy's grip.

Helga handed Ivy a small kettle and a warming plate. 'First, we'll need to create a hot poultice to apply to the site of the infection.' She pointed to Olivia's legs, which were red and bumpy. Ivy hadn't noticed that in the dim candlelight downstairs! *Ouch!*

Ivy used her closed coffin as a workstation, following Helga's directions to mix sagebrush, crushed rose thorn and orchid petals with a spoonful of pine-tree sap. She stirred it, letting it warm on the hot plate. Then, as Helga instructed, she brushed the ointment on to a bandage that Helga pressed against Olivia's legs.

'I'm impressed.' Helga nodded approvingly at

Ivy's work. 'Have you done this before?'

Ivy shook her head as she helped secure the compress, careful to control her super-strength so that she wouldn't hurt her sister. 'No, I don't know anything about vampire medicine.'

'Even more impressive. You have *natural* instincts. You could be a vampire healer one day.' Helga sniffed one of the medicine bottles before putting it away.

Horatio took a slight step forwards, leaning over Helga's shoulder to check their progress. 'Anything I can do?' he asked.

Helga waved him back. 'Not yet, not yet.' There was no room for a Frankenstein's monster-sized vampire in the mix; there was barely enough for Helga and Ivy.

Ivy helped the herbologist replace the caps on a set of silver bottles. 'I didn't know there even *were* vampire healers.'

'I didn't either.' Helga passed Ivy a pestle and

mortar and something that looked like catnip. 'Until I found my calling at Wallachia.'

Ivy stopped crushing the catnip. 'You went to Wallachia?'

Helga used a thermometer to check Olivia's temperature, nodding. 'It's a great place to learn vocational skills and find your passion. At least, it worked for *me*. It's not all pearls and snooty vamps, you know.' Helga winked. 'And even if you didn't want to pursue healing, Wallachia offers courses of study in any subject imaginable – with the highest standards of teaching.' She sat back on her heels, thinking. 'I remember when I was your age – so many possibilities.'

Ivy took a deep breath. 'Are you happy?' She handed back the crushed herb.

Helga smiled. 'It's my *calling*.' She sprinkled the herb on a fresh bandage. 'And now for the final touch.'

Ivy helped Helga apply a new poultice to

Olivia's legs. As if by magic, the colour started coming back into Olivia's cheeks and, seconds later, her eyelashes fluttered. Another moment passed and Olivia slowly opened her eyes. She looked at Ivy, who wanted to hold her hand as tightly as she could, but kept her grip gentle. Olivia was even more fragile than she'd thought!

'Welcome back, Miss Olivia. You should have told me you were human,' teased Helga. 'You gave us quite a scare!' She collected the rest of her bottles and ointments and stashed them back in her medicine bag.

'Oh.' Olivia looked confused. 'I thought it was obvious.' Ivy laughed.

'I'll give you two a moment,' said Helga.

'Thank you,' said Ivy.

Helga nodded and quietly started to leave them, Horatio in tow, while Ivy turned her attention back to Olivia. 'I'm so glad you're OK,' said Ivy, chipping at her Midnight Mauve nail varnish. 'Um . . . you were really sick, so I didn't know what you wanted me to do, but I was wondering . . . do you want me to call . . . *him*?'

Olivia stared at the ceiling.

I've said something wrong! Two seconds was all it took for me to make my sister feel rotten again! But then Olivia's lips parted and her face cracked into a big smile. She nodded in the direction of Helga, who was standing in the hallway outside their room with Horatio, chortling at something he'd said. Ivy hadn't heard him telling a joke!

'He finally got the courage.' Olivia was hoarse, but she sounded happy.

Ivy watched Helga and Horatio. Helga was brushing something off Horatio's lapel and straightening his tie. 'They are pretty cute together,' Ivy admitted.

'Don't tell me you've caught the wedding bug now too.' Olivia waggled her eyebrows. 'I'm sure a *certain somebody* would be pleased to hear you've found your soft side.'

Ivy shook her head, smiling. Her own wedding had never so much as crossed her mind, but she had to admit, Brendan *would* look handsome in a tux. She and Olivia watched the two vampires flirting and, although Ivy was not prepared to dive full-on into romance-o-mania, she couldn't help but look at Horatio and Helga and think: *Awww* . . .

This wedding stuff is going to kill me!

Olivia was in bed, tucked into her cool lavender sheets. She was finally starting to feel like herself again – although a much more exhausted version – and at least a hint of her usual pep had returned. All she needed was a good night's sleep.

Unfortunately, that gave her the energy to worry. No one had seen Tessa since the rehearsal dinner and Olivia was starting to fear they had an actual runaway bride on their hands. After all that Prince Alex and Tessa had overcome, was the wedding really going to fall apart?

I don't even know why Vincenzo turning up is such a shock! she thought. Obviously, he was over-the-top and insensitive and crass. But was that enough to make a bride flee her own rehearsal dinner, or for the twins' dad to tremble with fury? There was more to this than Olivia knew. But if Tessa really had done a runner . . . no bride meant no wedding! How dreadful! And who was going to tell Georgia that her big title story for *VAMP* magazine wasn't going ahead either? *I bet the designers have already started working on the cover!*

Maybe Olivia could leave *that* conversation to her sister . . .

A sliver of light appeared at the door, and Charles stuck his head into the room. 'How are you feeling, Olivia?'

Olivia propped herself up on her elbows. 'I'm

still breathing.'

'That's good to hear.' Olivia's bio-dad chuckled. He was wearing fluffy slippers and a shiny, black robe with a monogrammed *C* embroidered on it.

Ivy's coffin creaked open, like a zombie crawling out from the grave. 'Hey, are people still up?' she asked, sounding sleepy.

'I was just checking on your sister.' Charles opened the door wider and Ivy shielded her eyes from the light coming in from the hall. 'You should go back to bed.' He started to leave.

'Before you go, can I ask you a question?' Ivy bit her lip – as though she knew that she would have to tread carefully here. 'Would you mind telling us how you know Tessa's uncle? Olivia's little moment earlier meant that we never got to hear the full story.' Ivy grinned at her sister.

Charles entered the room and pulled out the chair from the desk. 'I guess you girls are old enough to know what happened.' He let out a long sigh as he settled into the chair. Olivia sat up straighter in her bed. She heard Ivy rearrange herself too.

'Very well then,' Charles began. 'Vincenzo and I were friends once, a long time ago. Best friends, actually, despite our differences. Vincenzo was always . . . an attention-seeker . . . but we got on despite his little scenes. Then we had a falling out. It's a long story that took place in a different era when the vampire rules were very different. His behaviour didn't just hurt me, but Tessa's family too. It made life very difficult for them, having someone in the family who generated so much gossip and rumour. Eventually, the stories became too much – he went too far. Tessa's family decided to have nothing more to do with him, and I argued with him. We never put aside our differences.' Olivia thought her bio-dad seemed tired, as if carrying around that grudge for all these years had been a heavy burden. 'If we hadn't let it fester for so long, we'd probably have it sorted out by now. But we didn't, and now it will forever be between us.'

Olivia gulped. Did she dare ask what her father had meant when he said Vincenzo would not ruin 'another wedding'?

'Dad,' Ivy started. 'What did you mean by –' As usual, her sister had got right to the point, but Charles anticipated what she was about to say and interrupted.

'Vincenzo was supposed to be the best man at my wedding.' Olivia caught her breath. She had never heard about her parents' wedding day. 'It was going to be a small service in America, very low-key and discreet. We'd asked Vincenzo to tell no one, because our relationship was largely a secret. But – as I'm sure you girls have seen – Vincenzo is a loud character and had an idea that he would invite all of our vampire friends over from Transylvania for a big party. Of course, word got out, and my parents discovered that I was planning to sneak off and marry your mother. My idea had been to get married and present Susannah to my mother and father as my wife. That way, they would have had no choice but to accept her. But, thanks to Vincenzo, my plans were ruined.'

'So you and Mom didn't get the wedding you wanted?' asked Olivia, after a quiet moment had passed.

'No.' Charles rubbed the ring he still wore on his left hand. 'But I did have a wonderful marriage, which is the most important thing. Vincenzo is partly correct. I'm not proud of the way I acted downstairs. I've had time to calm down and gain some perspective over the situation. At the very least, I hope you girls never behave like I did.' His eyebrows shot up as he looked at each of his daughters. Olivia nodded vigorously. 'But it is all in the past and there is no point in dwelling on it too much. Still, there are some friendships that can't be restored. Now –' he stood up – 'you two need to get to sleep.' Charles strode over and kissed both girls on the forehead. 'If the wedding goes ahead, you'll have another hectic day ahead of you tomorrow.'

Hectic I can handle, thought Olivia. *Just as long as I don't get another near-death experience!* She curled up in her bed, enjoying the soft hum of the ceiling fan. Her thoughts turned to Ivy's trip to Wallachia. The day had taken such a sharp turn, she'd never got a chance to ask her sister about the school visit! She peeked over the side of her bed at the sealed coffin. Her questions would have to wait until tomorrow. For now, her bio-dad was right. She needed to sleep . . .

Dong! Dong! Dong!

Olivia felt like she'd only been asleep for five minutes when a loud noise woke her.

Dong! Dong! Dong!

There it was again. She sat up. Ivy was already halfway out of the room, muttering, 'No, no, no!' Her sister tugged on the ends of her wild, slept-on hair. 'No!' she repeated.

'Now what?' asked Olivia, rubbing her face to try and wake herself up properly.

What was going on?

Chapter Nine

G*ooonnnnngggggg!* Ivy plugged her fingers into her ears as the metallic vibrations echoed through the castle. She had thought she was having a nightmare. She pinched herself, but the resounding noise still rang out. *It's . . . it's . . .* She suddenly recognised the sound. *The gong!* That could mean only one thing in Transylvania; she had learnt that at the Academy. *A duel!*

Ivy peered out of the bedroom door. 'Is there really another duel?' she shouted over the head-splitting racket. 'And, if so, what silly argument is it over *this* time?'

'What on earth is going on?' cried Olivia, as she scrambled down from the top bunk.

'I'll go check it out,' said Ivy, hastily tugging jeans on over her nightgown.

'Right behind you – well, sort of!' Olivia called as Ivy sprinted from the bedchamber and out of the castle on to the grounds. Even at full-speed, Olivia would have no chance of keeping up with a worried vampire!

Outside, the lush grass was wet and dewy under Ivy's toes. She spotted Vincenzo on the lawn. Of course, he *would* be the cause of all this commotion. He'd thrown his cape over one shoulder and he was standing with open arms, his face tilted up towards the castle. 'Karl Lazar!' he called through cupped hands. 'Karl Lazar! Come out!' Ivy's heart skidded to a stop. 'Let's settle this feud the old-fashioned way.' Vincenzo beat his fists against his chest.

A servant wearing white linen trousers and a

billowing shirt beat the gong again. Ivy waited, holding her breath. She hoped her father would ignore Vincenzo. Surely her dad wouldn't do something as barbaric as enter a duel. But then the massive doors of the castle swung open and Charles appeared in the archway.

Ivy's dad strode out, looking dignified in black trousers and a red silk shirt. Had the whole world gone batty? Olivia and Lillian followed closely behind him. Lillian was pulling the sash of her silk robe tight. Her porcelain face was screwed up with worry. Ivy didn't blame her. This was a terrible substitute for a wake-up call.

'Dad!' Ivy tugged on his sleeve as he passed her. 'You can't fight about this,' she begged. '*Please* don't fight.'

Lillian, resting a hand on his shoulder, piped up. 'Really, Charles, this is ridiculous. You can't honestly take *him* seriously.' She pointed at Vincenzo, who now seemed to be imitating a chicken pecking around the front lawn.

'Are you scared, Charles? Are you not enough of a vampire to follow vampire tradition?' Vincenzo was playing to the crowd that was slowly starting to gather out in front of the Lazars' home. The sunlight peeping over the castle roof was dazzling and the dry breeze gusting at their backs smelled of summer. Everything felt out of place for a duel. This was supposed to be the setting for Tessa's wedding day, not some macho death-match between two vamps old enough to know *so* much better!

Charles shook both Lillian and Ivy off, his jaw set. 'Don't worry. I'm not living in the Middle Ages.'

Olivia sidled up to Ivy and reached out for her hand, which Ivy took and tried not to crush.

From all over the castle, servants and courtiers streamed out on to the lawn. Ivy groaned. They looked just as excited as the students had at

Wallachia. But this was her *father*, not some dumb kid fighting over the rules of a stupid sport.

Vincenzo pointed a long finger at Charles. 'You embarrassed me in front of my niece.'

Charles casually placed his hands in his pockets, laughing. '*I* embarrassed you? I believe you embarrassed *yourself* by turning up looking like you were going to a fancy-dress party as Peter Cushing.'

'Who's Peter Cushing?' whispered Olivia.

'No idea,' Ivy whispered back.

Her dad narrowed his eyes. 'You have always caused problems, Vincenzo,' he continued, approaching the pony-tailed vampire slowly. 'Ever since we were at school, you've refused to grow up and act your age. What are you now, over two hundred years old? And yet you would rather play-act the scary villain than be a proper uncle to your niece, or a friend to me when I needed you.'

'I – that's not fair. I . . .' Vincenzo scratched his

cheek and shifted his weight from foot to foot.

Charles interrupted his sputtering. 'No, what isn't fair is that you make every major event about *you.*' He circled Vincenzo. 'My wedding, even your niece's – they become one big Vincenzo Show!'

'I do *not*!' Vincenzo pivoted in place, keeping his eyes on Charles. 'I mean, *they* do not!'

'Enough is enough, Vincenzo.' Charles folded his arms.

'But . . . but . . .' Then like a car with no petrol, Vincenzo stopped, dropping his greasy head. He clasped his hands together behind it, the way Ivy had seen boys at her school do when they missed an easy free-kick on the football pitch.

'You're right, my old friend,' Vincenzo said at last. 'Of course you're right – I came out here to make it up to Tessa and to try to do the right thing, but look at me. I've made a mess of everything all over again.'

Charles's posture softened. Ivy let out a breath

she hadn't realised she'd been holding. Was there still a chance she wouldn't have to witness another silly duel?

'I just didn't expect you would ever come back to Transylvania,' said Vincenzo. 'I thought I was safe living in a tiny village, being the centre of attention there. For years, it was enough for me. Then I heard that there was to be a royal wedding, I saw the newspaper reports – Tessa's photo and rumours of wedding guests, including you. I couldn't resist coming. I'm sorry.'

Ivy's father rested his hand on Vincenzo's shoulder. 'Apology accepted. You were right about what you said before – it's all in the past.'

Now that *is how vampires should act*, thought Ivy.

Prince Alex pushed his way through to the centre of the ring, his dark eyebrows drawn together. He looked as if he'd been getting ready for his wedding when the gong had struck. He already had his cummerbund fastened around his waist, but his sleeves were loose, awaiting some cufflinks. A flutter of hope sparked in Ivy's chest. *Maybe there will be a wedding, after all!*

'Speaking of the old ways –' Alex cleared his throat – 'what are we going to do about the duel? I'm pleased to see you two have made amends, but once a challenge has been issued, it cannot be refused.'

Charles ran his fingers through his hair, tilting his head. 'Says who, exactly?'

A young vampire stepped out of the crowd. 'How dare you talk to the Prince that way!'

Alex held up his hand. 'No, it's OK. Go on, Ka– *Charles*.'

Ivy's dad went on: 'Who says that we must follow through with a duel once the challenge has been issued? Who came up with these rules?'

Alex pursed his lips, looking as though he was trying to work out some particularly tricky maths problem in his head. 'I don't know. That's just how things have always been done.'

Charles looked back to Vincenzo. 'I am proud to be a vampire and I haven't turned my back on the old ways entirely, but that doesn't mean I think our system is perfect. Remember what Professor Igor taught us at Wallachia all those many years ago: *a person is on the right road in life when he walks it alone.*'

As soon as their dad finished, Olivia started clapping wildly. Every head turned in her direction. 'What?' she asked, shrinking back. 'Vampires don't applaud?'

Ivy laughed. She thought about what her father had said, how the right path was the one you created for yourself, and she realised she had never been more proud of her father. If her dad could graduate from the Academy without becoming a Wallachia drone, why couldn't she? Maybe it *would* be good for her. And, who knew – maybe she would be good for *it* too.

'Vincenzo.' Charles extended a hand to his old friend. Vincenzo hesitated but, after a moment, took the proffered palm. The two vampires pulled each other into a back-thumping hug. A cheer rose up from the crowd, but as fast as it had started, it died off.

Ivy followed the slowly turning heads, wondering what was drawing their attention. Then her heart sank to her toes.

Tessa was standing alone in the doorway.

Nobody moved. The tension stretched between the crowd and the former servant girl like a thick rubber band. Ivy waited, but nobody said anything. The silence felt more suspenseful than a horror movie! What was Tessa going to do – go on with the wedding or let her big day be ruined?

'Tessa.' Vincenzo advanced towards his niece, arms opened wide. But before he could get within a few feet of her, Tessa span around and dashed off across the grounds with her hair flying, running barefoot at a speed only a vampire could reach.

Ivy frowned at the fleeing figure. As far as she was concerned, Tessa was practically family. Almost like a third sister. Ivy tapped Olivia on the shoulder. 'Come on, I think this is a job for us.'

Olivia nodded. 'Twin sisters to the rescue.'

Olivia and Ivy slowed down when they saw Tessa. She was sitting on the edge of the rose meadow plucking grass from the ground and idly throwing it aside. Silently, they took a seat on either side of her and waited for her to talk.

Olivia rested her chin on her knees, staring out at the blues, purples and yellows that speckled the field. The fragrant mix of juniper and rose filled the air, making her feel peaceful for the first time in days.

'This is the first time I've seen my uncle in

years, you know. I've had nothing to do with him since I was a child, long before my father died.' Tessa twirled a blade of grass between her fingers. 'My family fell out with him when he made one scene too many. I began work at the palace and in time I almost forgot about the scandal he'd brought to our door. I fell in love with Alex and decided I just wouldn't mention my uncle to anyone. It would be better that way.' She rested her chin on her knees. 'But when he turned up yesterday I knew I couldn't escape my past any more. I know he seems nice enough now, but he's brought my family a lot of unhappiness.' She pressed her heels into the ground. 'And now he's doing it again! The Queen had finally learned to accept me – and then he showed up.'

Olivia saw Ivy shoot her a worried look. She also saw that Tessa had noticed it. 'You think I'm exaggerating,' Tessa went on, 'but it's true. Mark my words. Before the night is out, he'll have drunk too much O-Neg and be singing a stupid song, or who knows what other totally mortifying thing!'

Olivia giggled, then quickly tried to cover it up with a fake cough. 'Sorry,' she said when Tessa clearly wasn't buying the coughing routine. 'But I think families are *made* to be embarrassing. It's like their job. Trust me, I understand. My dad does tai chi in the front yard! Where the whole street can see him!' Tessa let out a soft snort. 'But listen to you.' Olivia gently touched the bride-to-be's arm. 'You're talking as if there *will* be a wedding now. That's progress.'

Tessa shook her head. 'I don't know. I'm worried that my uncle will make the Queen disapprove of me again. The Queen and I have come a long way, but Uncle Vincenzo doesn't exactly make my humble roots seem any more endearing. She already thinks I'm not good enough for Alex. This can only make things worse.'

'Is your uncle really a bad man, though, or

is he just sometimes a bit silly and OTT?' Olivia asked.

Tessa rolled her eyes. 'He's not bad exactly. You're right. He doesn't mean to do the things he does – he just gets a bit overexcited.'

'And don't you want the Queen to accept you for who you are?' Ivy said. 'I thought that was the whole point of this year's Valentine's Ball. You and Alex got together and you didn't have to change into some horrible, posh vampire, remember?' Ivy shuddered. 'I think we have enough of *those* running around. Vincenzo may be a little over-the-top . . .' Tessa raised one eyebrow. 'OK, a *lot* over-the-top and, well, he may be quite loud. In fact, he might be all the things you don't like. But he can work on being reliable and he can work on becoming a better uncle and *those* are the things that matter. So is it really that terrible if he acts a bit crazy in front of all these stuck-up vamps?'

'I guess not,' Tessa muttered.

'Trust me,' said Ivy, placing a hand on Tessa's shoulder. 'I know what it feels like to be the odd one out. You should see me surrounded by all those bunnies in Franklin Grove!' Tessa peered at her sideways, one corner of her mouth starting to curl up into a smile.

'It's not like it's going to kill them!' Olivia added. 'Only a wooden stake could do that.'

Ivy groaned at her sister's bad vampire joke, but Tessa grinned. 'I appreciate your optimism and all, but –' a mischievous look glimmered in her eye – 'don't come complaining to me when my uncle starts a conga!'

Olivia crossed her fingers and squeezed her eyes shut. 'Does this mean we're going to have a wedding? Does it?'

Tessa wrapped both the twins in a tight hug. 'It was never really off.'

'*Yes!* I knew it!' Olivia bounced up, squealing.

She checked her watch. 'But – oh my goodness – we don't have much time.' She was in business mode and her to-do list was already forming in her head.

Make-up

Hair

Nails

Jewellery

Avoid messy food at all costs . . .

'Right – we have to get to work.' Olivia snapped back to the present. 'First, we need to get dressed. Then Ivy needs to write some of her news article and, as for me, I have to . . .'

Olivia's words were swallowed by a fierce summer breeze that whipped through the grounds. The back of her neck tingled. From across the garden, she saw a single rose-head lift out of the meadow, floating on the warm air. Olivia couldn't see what colour it was, but she knew what she had to do. She ran after it, sprinting through the grass and clover. Without waiting, she plucked it from the air with both hands, too scared to look.

Tessa and Ivy arrived, panting. 'Well?' asked Ivy.

Slowly, as if holding a butterfly, Olivia uncurled her hands, revealing a perfect blue rose. 'Impossible love,' whispered Olivia.

Tessa gasped. 'Does that mean Alex and I – '

But Olivia cut her off. 'The rose isn't a message for you and Alex. You two are perfect together.' She stared at the rose, transfixed. 'It's a message for me and Jackson.'

Chapter Ten

Glowing paper lanterns and fairy lights flickered high above the dance floor where a ten-piece vampire band was playing an upbeat version of Beethoven's *Symphony No. 5*. Deep-purple blooms spilled out of the towering centerpieces that were balanced on top of plush velvet tablecloths so expensive looking Ivy couldn't imagine actually *eating* off them.

The wedding had gone off without a hitch. Tessa looked beautiful in her lace dress and Alex had seemed fit to burst when he saw her walking down the aisle. Even the Queen had appeared pleased! The choir sang from a balcony and four little girls scattered flower petals in front of Tessa's satin slippers as she walked down the thick carpet towards the prince she was about to marry, on the arm of – Vincenzo! After Olivia's little speech Tessa must have found him to make up with him. Ivy couldn't wait to find out the details.

Then there had been the vows; the rings; the first kiss as a married couple. Even Ivy had been moved – not to *tears* or anything, but still, it had been sweet. Olivia had teased Ivy that she'd been crying, but she seriously wasn't. Her nose was just itchy.

After Olivia had caught her blue rose, a big yellow one had come and whacked Ivy in the face, giving her a nose full of pollen. She'd be sneezing for a week. Ivy pulled the yellow rose out of her bag, smoothing the petals. She knew the colour yellow meant 'new beginnings', but did it have to mean watery eyes and the sniffles too? *OK, Universe.* Ivy lifted her eyes to the dark, night sky. *You're coming in loud and clear.* Everything seemed to be telling her to go to Wallachia Academy – but how could she leave Olivia and Brendan, especially now, when her sister seemed to need her most?

Ivy took a seat next to Olivia at one of the round guest tables. Olivia was dressed in a gorgeous pink chiffon gown, her hair pulled back with a shimmery headband. The twins sat in silence, watching Alex and Tessa share their first dance to the *Moonlight Sonata.* Tessa's dress was a stunning lace gown adorned with silk and tulle roses. Buttons lined the back of it, all the way from the neckline to the elegant train that trailed lightly upon the floor. Alex twirled his new bride around the dance floor, dipping her low and planting a sweet kiss on her cheek.

'Now that,' Ivy insisted, 'is cheesy.'

Olivia turned to face her, pinching Ivy's cheeks and tugging at them like she was a long lost aunt at a family reunion. 'I know there is a hopeless romantic hiding somewhere behind that tough goth exterior.'

Ivy put her hands on her hips and gave her sister a 'try me' look. 'Are you sure about that?' Olivia rolled her eyes. Ivy smoothed down her black kimono-style dress and adjusted the chopsticks that were pinning her bun in place.

The music stopped and Prince Alex took the microphone. 'We would like to thank each and every one of you for making our special day possible.' Ivy noticed him wink at the two of them. 'It is my great honour to present to you my bride, *Princess* Tessa!' The crowd cheered. Tessa was wearing a delicate tiara on top of her elegant up-do. 'And now, we'd like to invite you, our guests, to join us on the dance floor.' He handed the microphone back to the lead singer and the band started up again.

Olivia raised the lens of her camera and

snapped a few shots. Their article for *VAMP* magazine was due first thing Monday morning and Ivy still had a small pad of paper stashed in her purse for jotting down final notes. *A Date with Destiny – Transylvania's Very Own Cinderella Story*, the headline would read. She hoped Georgia would eat it up.

'Oh my darkness!' Ivy grabbed Olivia. 'Look over there!' She pointed at the head table, where Vincenzo was offering his hand to the Queen.

Ivy covered her mouth in horror – and a little amusement. The Queen stared, blinking at Vincenzo's outstretched hand. To Ivy's surprise, Her Majesty accepted his invitation. She even managed not to look totally appalled. Ivy's father was dancing with Lillian nearby, leading her in swift steps to the band's tempo – Ivy could tell he was doing everything he could to take her in the opposite direction of Vincenzo's flailing dance moves. Vincenzo was twirling around to the song like he was performing an act in the *Nutcracker*. Meanwhile, the Queen looked terribly confused and was just shuffling from side to side snapping her fingers. That was bad enough, but if Vincenzo managed to force the Queen into a conga line, Ivy thought she might literally die laughing!

Tessa tapped her mother-in-law on the shoulder. 'Mind if I cut in, Your Majesty?' Her new tiara sparkled under the twinkly lights.

The Queen fanned herself, a bright flush on her porcelain cheeks. 'Be my guest!' she said and scurried away as quickly as if someone had pulled the fire alarm.

Olivia flattened her hand over her heart, pointing to Tessa and Vincenzo. 'Oh my goodness!'

Tessa curtsied in front of her uncle, who bowed in return and looked like he might almost burst with pride. 'Shall we?' asked Tessa. The uncle–niece duo waltzed around the floor, eyes shining and big smiles stretched across their faces.

'Are you two behaving?' Ivy and Olivia tilted their chins back to see their father standing behind them. His tie was loose around his neck and his sleeves were rolled up. He must have really been dancing up a storm!

'Of course,' they said together. Lillian pulled a chair up next to the girls, whipping a mirror out of her clutch bag and smoothing her hair back into place with a pocket-sized comb.

Ivy twisted in her seat. 'You know, Dad, it was pretty cool what you did today.'

'You act surprised.' Charles frowned. 'I'm cool. I'm hip.' He turned on the spot, modelling his admittedly very suave-looking tuxedo.

Ivy mock-scowled at him. 'Dad, the most recent music you listen to comes from the eighteenth century. But anyway, we're proud of you for letting go of past grudges.'

Lillian stood back up, looping her arm through

Charles's. 'Proud, indeed.' She planted a gentle kiss on his cheek and Ivy tried not to giggle when her father's face blushed three shades redder. The two excused themselves to take a stroll around the grounds and Ivy and Olivia waved them off.

'I haven't seen Dad this happy in ages.' Ivy sighed, leaning back in her chair. Wedding guests passed by, balancing plates full of red-velvet cake and strawberries dripping with chocolate fondue.

In an unoccupied corner of the dance floor, Ivy spotted Helga and Horatio. Helga's arms were stretched stiffly around Horatio's thick neck and they were swaying a foot apart, out of step with the music. And there was the wedding planner, deep in conversation with a handsome man as she led him around the flower arrangements, pointing out the most spectacular stems.

'I think Lucia's luck could be on the turn,' Ivy said. 'And check out Helga and Horatio!' She bounced in her seat, casting an excited look at Olivia, but her sister was staring down at the bright-blue rose she'd been carrying around since the moment she'd caught it.

Ivy reached over and squeezed her sister's hand. 'I've made a decision. I'm not –'

Olivia held up her hand. 'Yes, Ivy . . . you *are*.'

'But I don't want to leave you.'

Olivia looked at Ivy seriously. 'I can survive a school year. Yes, it'll bite – but it's worth it, isn't it? You need to find out more about your heritage, and about yourself. Your life as a vampire won't always include me and I'm OK with that.'

Suddenly, Ivy wasn't convinced that they'd been born only minutes apart. Olivia seemed so mature! She wrapped her sister up in a huge hug, and not just to hide the tears pooling in her eyes – though that was an added benefit.

'Ouch!' Olivia yelped. 'Watch the super-strength!'

Ivy softened her embrace. 'Oops! Guess it's

a good thing I'm going to Wallachia after all.' She pulled away and poked at her bicep. 'I really need to get these freaky vamp powers under control.' Ivy felt her phone vibrate from inside her black clutch. She pulled it out. 'It's Brendan,' she told Olivia.

'Well, go on then.' Olivia shooed her away. Ivy really did have the most understanding sister in the world – of humans or vampires.

Ivy picked up the hem of her dress and walked out into the shadowy grounds, beyond the gleam of the paper lanterns and loud music. 'Hello?' She plugged one ear with a finger so she could hear better.

'You answered!' Brendan's voice was husky and familiar and made Ivy's heart ache in her chest. 'How's the wedding?'

Ivy swallowed hard. 'It's been . . . eventful,' she admitted with a short laugh.

'What's wrong? You sound all weird and

scratchy.' Her boyfriend knew her too well.

'Brendan,' she felt herself waver but then remembered what Olivia had said about getting to know her heritage and getting to know herself. 'I think I'm going to stay in Transylvania and go to Wallachia for a while.' A long pause stretched between them like the Atlantic Ocean. 'Um, are you still there?' she asked.

'Yeah. I'm still here. And I think that's exactly what you need to do, Ivy,' said Brendan. She could tell that he meant it. 'But on one condition.'

Ivy's forehead wrinkled. 'What's that?'

'Don't you dare come back to Franklin Grove all snooty,' he said, teasing. 'Or your sister and I will have to knock you down a peg or two.'

'Please,' Ivy replied. 'You two couldn't knock me anywhere. It's my super-vampy powers that got me into this mess in the first place, remember.' Ivy tried to joke, but even as she said it she was almost overwhelmed at the thought of her family getting on the plane without her. She'd be staying here and Brendan would be waiting for her there, in Franklin Grove. What if she hated Wallachia? The only person she knew there was Petra, and she wasn't so sure that girl could be trusted. Sophia, Camilla, Brendan, Olivia – she already had the best friends anyone could ask for. All of these changes were too much to bear. 'It's just that I'm really going to miss you,' she admitted. 'Even more than I realised. Coming to Transylvania has made me see how difficult it will be.'

She heard Brendan gasp. 'Did Ivy Vega just get all sappy on me?'

Ivy knew her boyfriend couldn't see her fist planted firmly on her left hip, but she hoped he would sense it, and get the point. 'You better not tell a soul.'

'Cross my heart.' Brendan chuckled. 'But, for the record . . . I'll miss you too.'

After they had said their goodbyes – maybe

three or four times more than was necessary – Ivy clicked her phone shut and stuffed it back into her elegant but too-tiny bag. *Smeared eyeliner would most definitely not be a good look*, she thought, swiping underneath her eyes.

When she re-entered the hall, her eyes locked with Olivia's. Her sister was waiting with her patented Olivia smile and open arms.

'Don't forget about me, OK?' Ivy said, hugging her twin.

'Hello?' Her sister fake-slapped her. 'How could I? Whenever I look in the mirror, I'm reminded of you. We're identical, remember?'

'Except for the blusher.'

'And the extra eyeliner.'

The girls giggled, before their sweet moment was broken by a single word: *Paaarty!*

Vincenzo pumped his fist on the dance floor and jumped into a split mid-air.

'Ouch!' Both girls cringed in unison. There

was the sound of fabric tearing. 'That looked like it hurt.'

The wedding band sped up the number and vampires dressed in their evening best flocked to the dance floor. *When in Rome . . .* thought Ivy, as she dragged Olivia out after her.

'Let's dance!'

Two conga lines, a vamp sing-a-long, and a good old boogie to 'Let's Do the Vamp Walk', and Olivia was worn out. She wandered out of the dance hall, breathless. She'd been cheering at football games for years, but these vamps had party stamina! She stopped in the archway to watch everyone dance to 'A Hard Day's Bite'.

Olivia looked from Ivy to her dad and Lillian, and finally to her grandparents, who were bopping away like they were two hundred years younger than they really were. These people were her family and maybe, just maybe, she'd be OK without . . . She forced herself to think the name.

Jackson.

She strolled along the outside passageway that ran along the edge of the mansion. Crickets were chirping and Olivia could just make out the Big Dipper if she ducked her head out into the open air.

Voices were coming from an adjoining room. 'The bats *have* to be ready for their release at ten sharp!' Olivia overheard Lucia the wedding planner directing. 'The couple simply cannot leave without a flock to herald their new start. It's bad luck not to have bats!'

Olivia chuckled to herself. *Vamps! They have some crazy traditions.* She walked along, appreciating the gardens and the starry night, the soft grass sinking under her high heels. The night was so tranquil that she was startled by the sound of her phone beeping.

She pulled it out of her clutch bag. The screen

glowed green, looking radioactive in the darkness. Her heart flip-flopped. It was a text. From *him*.

Miss you xoxo

Olivia hugged the phone to her chest. Maybe the rose was wrong. Blue could mean all sorts of things, right? Since when did it mean 'impossible love', anyway? Plus, Olivia wasn't a vampire, she was human. The Free Rose of Summer might work differently for her. It was possible. *Perhaps . . .*

Olivia plucked a pink primrose from one of the flower beds and held it up to her nose. Pink *was* more her colour, after all. As she wandered the grounds outside, a funny feeling started to take over. She felt light, happy even. Sure, Jackson was far away and had his exciting movie career, and Ivy was leaving her to start a new school – but perhaps there were new opportunities ahead for Olivia too.

Who knows? she thought. *Maybe this just means it's time for me to focus on . . . me!*

TWIN TALK!

In this exciting new interview, VAMP magazine's Georgia Huntingdon gets the inside scoop on the wedding of the year – from the twins who made it happen!

Georgia Huntingdon: Wow, where to begin? The gossip columns have gone into total overdrive! OK, first thing – is it true that you guys stopped the runaway bride?

Ivy Vega: She was hardly a runaway bride! Tessa – er, I mean, the Princess – only went to the garden to get some air. There was a bit of a ruckus on the day of the wedding, you see, so we went to talk to her. It was never really off.

Georgia: A ruckus? That sounds exciting! Were there punches thrown?

Ivy: No, no violence . . .

Georgia: A sword fight at sunset?

Ivy: More like incredibly bad dancing.

Georgia: Well, what was it, then?

Ivy: Princess Tessa's uncle turned up out of the blue. No one had seen him in a long time and things were a bit strained at first, but everyone got over it. I think it was the perfect ending actually, especially after the hectic preparations!

Georgia: Oh yes, I heard about those! Olivia, darling, is it true you made the wedding planner *cry*?

Olivia Abbott: That's an exaggeration!

Georgia: So you *did*?

Olivia: Er . . . kind of. She was upset about something and I came to the rescue. I certainly didn't *mean* to make her cry! We left on good terms though.

Georgia: What about your brush with death?

Olivia: I took some vampire medicine by accident after I fell into a patch of Bloodbite Nettles! That was scary.

Georgia: So you weren't bitten by a giant snake or attacked by out-of-control wedding bats?

Olivia: No! Where did you hear that? Wow, the grapevine's *really* inaccurate.

Ivy: Ooh, I've got an even better one. I read yesterday that you grew an extra head after eating too much wedding cake. I don't think vampires understand bunnies at all! I mean, you can't die from having two heads.

Olivia: Besides, I've already got one. It's called Ivy and it never stops talking!

Ivy: Very funny. But seriously, what would you do without me?

Georgia: Yes, what *will* you do without her? Ivy, I've heard that you definitely want to take your place at the prestigious Wallachia Academy. No offence, but it doesn't seem like your cup of B-neg.

Ivy: I just think it's time for a change. School's pretty important, and besides, I can take some really exciting courses in writing to help with my career! But seriously – if it's a total bore I'm sure I can shake it up a little.

Georgia: Watch out, Wallachia: Ivy Vega's coming!

Ivy: Exactly. I'll definitely miss everyone though, especially Olivia. And Brendan, of course. But they're both totally cool about it, they're really supportive – and I'll make sure they look after each other!

Georgia: So what's next? Tales of midnight feasts in the dorm rooms? Classroom pranks?

Ivy: I can hardly tell you that! All the fun would go out of it. Everyone knows you need the element of surprise.

Georgia: Ah, so there *will* be some fun. I'm sure our

readers can't wait to hear what you get up to. The hottest star at the best vampire school in the world – brilliant! Will you be dropping the black eye shadow for red socks and pleated skirts, then?

Ivy & Olivia: *No way!*

Georgia: Guess that's settled then. [Laughs] OK, girls, it was great speaking to you. And if Olivia grows any extra limbs, you know where to come.

Olivia: Don't hold your breath!

In the next VAMP magazine interview with the vampire community's favourite twins, Georgia hears about Ivy and Olivia's latest exploits – don't forget to put it in your diary!

EGMONT PRESS: ETHICAL PUBLISHING

Egmont Press is about turning writers into successful authors and children into passionate readers – producing books that enrich and entertain. As a responsible children's publisher, we go even further, considering the world in which our consumers are growing up.

Safety First
Naturally, all of our books meet legal safety requirements. But we go further than this; every book with play value is tested to the highest standards – if it fails, it's back to the drawing-board.

Made Fairly
We are working to ensure that the workers involved in our supply chain – the people that make our books – are treated with fairness and respect.

Responsible Forestry
We are committed to ensuring all our papers come from environmentally and socially responsible forest sources.

For more information, please visit our website at www.egmont.co.uk/ethical

Egmont is passionate about helping to preserve the world's remaining ancient forests. We only use paper from legal and sustainable forest sources, so we know where every single tree comes from that goes into every paper that makes up every book.

This book is made from paper certified by the Forestry Stewardship Council (FSC®), an organisation dedicated to promoting responsible management of forest resources. For more information on the FSC, please visit **www.fsc.org**. To learn more about Egmont's sustainable paper policy, please visit **www.egmont.co.uk/ethical**.